'Madison, I want you, all of you... to you...'

She frowned up at him as if he were speaking a foreign language, a language that she'd barely even started to grasp. But occasional words filtered through, and despite her utter confusion somehow she understood what it was Guy was saying—because she wanted to get close to him, too, wanted to get to know him, all of him. She stared back at his gorgeous face, and for a slice of time it almost seemed possible that with a man like Guy maybe she could work it out, maybe they could learn this language together.

Carol Marinelli recently filled in a form where she was asked for her job title and was thrilled, after all these years, to be able to put down her answer as writer. Then it asked what Carol did for relaxation and after chewing her pen for a moment Carol put down the truth—writing. The third question asked—what are your hobbies? Well, not wanting to look obsessed or, worse still, boring, she crossed the fingers on her free hand and answered swimming and tennis. But, given that the chlorine in the pool does terrible things to her highlights and the closest she's got to a tennis racket in the last couple of years is watching the Australian Open—I'm sure you can guess the real answer!

Recent titles by the same author:

CHRISTMAS ON THE CHILDREN'S WARD
SPANISH DOCTOR, PREGNANT NURSE
(Mediterranean Doctors)
UNDERCOVER AT CITY HOSPITAL
(Police Surgeons)

NEEDED:
FULL-TIME FATHER

BY
CAROL MARINELLI

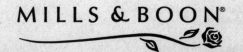

First published in Great Britain 2005
Paperback Edition 2006
Harlequin Mills & Boon Limited,
Eton House, 18-24 Paradise Road, Richmond, Surrey TW9 1SR

© The SAL Marinelli Family Trust 2005

ISBN 0 263 84710 1

Set in Times Roman 10½ on 13½ pt.
03-0206-44730

Printed and bound in Spain
by Litografia Rosés, S.A., Barcelona

CHAPTER ONE

HER very own parking space!

Pulling on the handbrake of her smart, practical and incredibly clean sedan, Madison Walsh took a moment out of her busy schedule to indulge herself, staring with quiet satisfaction at the writing on the wall.

RESERVED / ED NUM

OK, it didn't say reserved for Madison Walsh, Nursing Unit Manager, Accident and Emergency Department, it didn't even matter that a parking space was possibly the last thing a perpetually early-for-everything woman like Madison needed—but it was hers!

Another step in the right direction, another life goal achieved.

Locking her car, Madison waved as Gerard Dalton slid his dark blue car into his own reserved parking spot and waited politely as the elderly gentleman climbed out.

'One day I'll beat you to work!' Gerard grinned. 'You're not due to start for another two hours, Madison.'

'Neither are you,' Madison pointed out, walking with

Gerard through the dark car park, bypassing the darkened accident and emergency entrance and heading instead to the main reception area of the hospital.

'I guess we both just want to have that one final check before it's all systems go. Mind you,' he added rather more lightly, 'not before a good strong cup of coffee. Let's hope the kitchen staff remembers that we're here and delivers us some milk…' His voice trailed off as Madison held up a carrier bag.

'I stopped at the garage, just in case there wasn't any.'

'Of course you did,' Gerard said with a wry note to his voice. 'Who's looking after that gorgeous daughter of yours while her mother's out all hours?'

'Emily's fine.' Madison laughed. 'She's having a sleepover at my friend Helen's, so that I could be here early today.'

'And she's enjoying going to school?'

'She loves it,' Madison responded warmly, as they arrived outside the deserted reception area. She nodded her thanks as the security guard gave a thumbs-up and the doors slid open.

'Morning, Vic!'

'Morning, Professor, morning, Sister,' Vic responded cheerfully. 'All ready for the big day?'

'I hope so,' Madison said, rolling her eyes. 'If we're not, we're about to find out the hard way.'

'How could we not be ready?' Gerard said assuredly as they walked along the highly polished corridor and into the vacant emergency unit. 'We've been planning this day for months now.'

'I know,' Madison sighed, flicking on lights as she went, noticing how hard the domestic staff had been working in the last couple of days, every last trace of builders' dust gone. The plastic wraps had been removed from the chairs in the waiting room, even the vending machines had been stocked up, but nothing could take away the scent of new paint and carpeting, and the pristine look of a hospital that had yet to see a patient. 'At least that's what I keep telling myself, but I've been awake every night for the past week, thinking of a million and one things that might go wrong.'

'You worry too much,' Gerard admonished, steering her away from the empty nurses' station and into the staffroom. 'You're the most meticulous, organised person I know, Madison. That's one of the reasons I insisted on having you as the NUM when they offered me the director's role for the new accident and emergency department. Designing a hospital from scratch is a hard enough task, but without a well-run, functioning emergency department…' He paused for a moment, kettle poised in mid-fill, and Madison noted he'd pulled out three mugs, which summed Gerard Dalton up in a heartbeat.

He'd be making a brew for Vic as well—porter or professor, it didn't matter. If you were on Gerard's team, you belonged.

'You know this is one of the proudest days of my life.'

'There'd be a lot of proud moments in a life like yours, Gerard,' Madison said warmly, and if it sounded gushing she didn't care. Gerard Dalton was quite simply the finest doctor and the most honourable man she had ever met. A devoted husband and father, he had somehow managed to squeeze in a career that would have anyone reeling. As well as being an esteemed emergency doctor, he was also a tireless AID worker for developing countries. The long list of letters after his name had been extremely well earned and, always thrilled to work alongside him, Madison had been honoured when he'd hand-picked her to join him in the daunting task of getting the accident and emergency department of the brand new Heatherton Hospital up and hopefully running successfully.

'There have been a lot of proud moments,' Gerard agreed. 'But this is something really special. I don't know how many times I've said in my career that if only things were different, if only we had the right equipment, if only someone had thought to put that here or this there…' He gave an apologetic smile. 'I'm waffling.'

'No, you're not,' Madison said. 'I've been thinking exactly the same thing—all this wonderful new equipment, consultations with the designers, hand-picking the staff, it's going to be wonderful.'

'If you like that sort of thing.' Gerard smiled and Madison did, too. 'You either love hospitals or you hate them, I guess. What time do you think the staff will start getting here?'

'Well, no one's actually due to start until seven, but everyone was so enthusiastic when they came for orientation, I'm sure they'll start trickling in after six.'

'And the department officially opens at nine?' Gerard checked his paperwork and Madison smothered a smile—they'd been over and over the details a thousand times, but despite Gerard's amazing ability to retain anything remotely medical, when it came to trivial matters such as clocks, budgets or even where he'd put down his glasses, he was the original absent-minded professor.

'We open at nine for patients making their own way in, but we're closed to ambulances until eleven a.m., which will give us a couple of hours to iron out any minor hiccups that might arise.'

'Good idea,' Gerard agreed.

'It was *your* idea, Gerard,' Madison said, not bothering to hide her smile this time.

'So it was,' Gerard said. 'Right, it looks like all we need now is a patient.'

'And a consultant,' Madison added, instantly regretting the slight edge to her voice. Because she'd worked alongside Gerard for so many years now, naturally he picked up on it.

'You're going to like him, Madison. Guy Boyd is the finest doctor I've had the privilege to work with.' Which, coming from Gerard, was high praise indeed, but still Madison remained hesitant.

'I just wish I'd met him. From what you've described, he's not exactly…' Her voice trailed off, not wanting to be rude, not wanting to judge before she'd even laid eyes on the man, but Gerard spoke for her.

'Guy's a bit of a free spirit,' Gerard said, and no

doubt he meant well, but the description of the new consultant brought absolutely no comfort to Madison, the words 'free spirit' searing through her like dental pain as she gritted her teeth. 'He just doesn't like to be tied down in one place for too long.'

'He doesn't like responsibility, you mean?' Madison responded. 'Look, I'll reserve judgement till I've met him, Gerard, but we've known each other long enough to be honest, and the truth of the matter is I'm not particularly keen on "free spirits" wandering around my department. I want fully grounded, on-the-ball, committed workers.'

'I know,' Gerard answered, smiling placidly at Madison's frown. 'And I know we've both been in on every interview, that we've both agreed on every member of the team, but in Guy's case he simply couldn't get here because he was overseas. When I emailed him about the new department I couldn't believe my luck—*our* luck—when he said that he was keen to be a part of it.'

'But he's only prepared to commit to a six-month contract,' Madison pointed out. 'We're aiming for continuity, Gerard, staff who will follow the vision…'

'We are.' Gerard nodded. 'And if it was anyone else I'd have said no but, believe me, six months with Guy Boyd on board is too good to pass up. You're just going to have to trust me, Madison.'

'Which I do,' Madison said, forcing a smile, determined to let nothing mar this day. 'I'm probably overreacting. I'm sure that he'll turn out to be great.'

'Once you get used to him,' Gerard added, and Madison wished he hadn't! 'Guy's not exactly into hospital politics. He's not exactly politically correct—very much his own man,' Gerard explained, but seeing Madison's tight expression hastily turned his back and spooned sugar into a mug. 'I'd best take this out to Vic. I noticed the sign diverting patients has been taken down. We ought to put it back up until the department officially opens.'

'Gerard, when you say he's not into hospital politics…' Madison didn't even finish her sentence, her audience lost as Gerard headed off for an extended chat with Vic. Madison headed through the department towards the entrance, picking up the sign the cleaners must have taken down when they'd polished the doors. She pressed it back against the glass, and jumped as a looming shadow appeared out of the darkness.

'We're closed,' Madison mouthed, pointing to the sign, but perhaps in the subdued light she couldn't be seen. It was either a patient who needed help or a member of staff, so Madison tapped the window and gestured to Reception. 'Go that way,' she said, exaggerating the words to make herself understood, peering into the bleak ambulance bay.

He didn't look like a patient. Certainly, from his relaxed stance he wasn't in any pain, although admittedly all she could really see was a white T-shirt. But there wasn't any urgency in his actions.

'Problem?' Gerard asked, coming behind her and flicking on the light, which reduced Madison's visibility to zero.

'Either an eager patient or a keen member of staff.'

'We can deal with both.' Gerard gave a half laugh and, cupping his hands, pressed them against the window.

'Why, it's Guy!' The delight in his voice forced Madison's attention and she watched as Gerard fiddled with the door. 'Can't we open it?'

'Not without Security,' Madison answered, resisting the urge to cup her own hands against the glass and have a good look at the new, *politically incorrect* consultant, but curiosity got the better of her and, cupping her own hand against the glass, she peered out into the pre-dawn darkness. Her eyes squinted to focus then she stepped back as a smiling, utterly laid-back face greeted hers. Inexplicably she felt as if he was way, way too close to her, his presence definitely felt even though he was safely on the other side of a thick glass door. In that split second a shooting flame of something she couldn't quite define rippled through her—and had Madison pulling away rapidly, catching her breath as if she'd been stung.

'Are you OK?'

'Fine,' Madison answered briskly. 'He'll have to walk round to Reception. We should go and meet him…' She headed off, expecting Gerard to follow her. After all, despite her own misgivings about his employment, it was the new consultant that was arriving and he deserved to be greeted. But as she walked back through the sterile waiting room it took a moment to realise she was walking alone.

'Gerard?' Turning with a smile, Madison stared back to where she'd just come from and froze. She stood fixed to the spot. Vaguely aware of the coffee from her cup splashing onto the new blue carpet, followed in a split second by the sound of the cheap, china mug thudding to the ground, the world moved in slow motion for a moment. A tiny, useless croak came from her throat and then she was running, running towards her boss, her friend, her confidant, running as fast as her legs would carry her, as Gerard slowly slid down the length of the glass door, his face in the fluorescent light a hideous purple. Then the world was speeding up again, seemingly stuck on fast-forward, and Madison begged it to slow back down as she reached her boss, broke his leaden fall a touch and lowered Gerard to the floor.

Madison crouched on her knees, willing herself to hold it together, drawing on her professionalism, almost reading off the chart that was tattooed in her mind, through the ABC—airway, breathing, circulation—trying, *trying* to treat him as a patient, desperate to give back to this amazing, talented man some of what he'd so readily delivered to others in the course of his career.

'It's OK, Gerard,' Madison soothed him, her voice amazingly assured. She checked his airway, watching, praying to see the rise and fall of his chest as her fingers desperately fought to locate a pulse in his neck.

'Gerard.' Her voice was sharper now, tears muffling her words as she called out his name, but even as she pinched his nose, tried to keep her breathing even enough to drag in some air to exhale, clamped trembling fingers into position over his chest, Madison knew he had gone, knew in that moment the vital, eloquent, disarming man had already gone for ever.

But that knowledge didn't stop her from trying to bring him back to them all—to his family that needed him, to his friends and colleagues that adored him, to the department he had created from the first blueprint.

Barely looking up as footsteps thudded towards her, she noted with relief that the new consultant had picked up vital emergency equipment on his way—an ambu-bag to reinflate Gerard's lungs and a mini oxygen cylinder, even the red bag that contained a self-administering defibrillator. She moved aside as the man she'd briefly glimpsed ripped open the packages, connected the tubing and took over Gerard's airway with an ambu-bag. She concentrated instead on cardiac compressions as Vic arrived, shouting into his walkie-talkie for assistance, dragged an oxygen cylinder over and connected it to the bag Guy was squeezing.

'What happened?' Guy's voice was deep but urgent—no introduction, no niceties, because there was *nothing* nice about this.

'You saw what happened,' Madison answered, leaning in as she pummelled Gerard's chest. 'He just collapsed.'

'Did he complain of chest pain?'

'No.'

'Headache, dizziness, shortness of breath?'

'Nothing!' She almost shouted it. 'I thought he was walking behind me.'

'Is there anything else I can do?' It was Vic speaking now, Vic desperate to help, to do something, anything. 'I let Switchboard know on my walkie-talkie as I was running over. The nursing supervisor was just pulling up in the car park when it happened, they're going to send for her.'

'We need to get him to Resus—get a trolley,' Guy shouted, but Vic was already picking up Gerard's shoulders, and Guy assisted him, somehow carrying the leaden weight. Madison raced ahead, turning on machines that had so far only been used in practice runs, completely unable to comprehend that the patient they'd so eagerly anticipated, had so long awaited, had trained and practiced for, had, in fact, turned out to be Gerard himself.

As Madison ripped open chest pads, Guy tore at Gerard's suit then picked up the chest paddles and placed them over Gerard's chest to give a reading of his heart rate.

'Asystole,' Madison said, seeing the flat line appear on the monitor. She plugged in the ambu-bag to the walled oxygen and commenced the breathing for Gerard, but Guy shook his head.

'It could be fine VF,' he said, hoping that the reading that was showing on the monitor wasn't a true one—asystole was the worse kind of cardiac arrest, but there was a chance, a tiny one, that his heart was fibrillating and that the reading was so fine the machine couldn't pick it up, a tiny chance that he had a type of cardiac arrhythmia that could be reverted and Madison stood back as Guy gave Gerard the benefit of the doubt and delivered a shock to his lifeless body.

'Still asystole.' Guy's voice was hoarse. 'Keep up the massage.' They needed more hands, needed help here now, and thankfully it arrived. Shirley, the nursing supervisor, racing into Resus, her expression appalled when she took in the scene.

'Bag him, Shirley,' Madison ordered, clipping a tourniquet to Gerard's flaccid arm and getting IV access as Guy continued to pound Guy's chest. 'Vic, call for an ambulance, tell them we need the MICA.'

'MICA?' Vic gave a panicked, bewildered shake of his head.

'The mobile intensive care unit, Switch will understand. Tell them to say that our doctor has had a cardiac arrest and we need him to be transferred, we need an ICU bed…' Madison was pulling up the standard drugs used during a cardiac arrest and handing them to Guy, before he even had to name them. She winced as he shocked Gerard again, the horrible, singed smell filling the sterile room. She felt the indignity of seeing the immaculate Gerard with his chest bared, his tie cut and pushed to the side. But as was so much the man, a handkerchief still peeped out of his suit pocket—a poignant reminder of the immaculate man they were trying to save.

'Look, I don't know if it means anything,' Vic spoke, his voice shaky, unsure of his reception, but Guy was open to any suggestion and nodded urgently for Vic to go on. 'He said something about a sore back last night when he went home.'

'He could have a ruptured aortic aneurysm,' Guy said, referring to a dire surgical emergency where the main artery of the body ruptured.

'He strained his back, moving a box with me, last night,' Madison said, shaking her head. 'I was there, Guy. It was a simple strain, I saw it happen myself…'

'Open a thoracotomy tray,' Guy called, and almost on autopilot Madison went to retrieve one. She set it up to open Gerard's chest, to rip through his sternum so that Guy could visualise the heart, massage it with his hands, clamp the aorta, tie off a bleed or remove a clot, do something, anything, that might prolong this wonderful life. But all Madison knew was that Gerard wouldn't have wanted it.

'We did everything we could.'

She'd heard it said so many times, had used the sentence herself on many, many occasions, but maybe for the first time Madison knew exactly what it meant. That sometimes to do everything you actually had to be brave and do nothing—because nothing modern medicine had to offer was going to help now. Despite heroics, despite best effort, nothing could make a difference for Gerard—certainly not ripping open his chest with a saw.

'He's gone.' She couldn't believe she was saying it, yet she knew that it was true. Knew that going on even a moment longer was an indignity, that Professor Gerard Dalton had gone and nothing was going to bring him back.

'He might have…' For a second Guy wavered, torn

between hope and truth, and for the first time Madison actually looked at him, took in the man she'd never formally met but who seemed somehow to understand the atrocity of what had taken place. Dark blond hair flopped over his forehead, the same raw anguish she had first witnessed when he had knelt down beside Gerard's lifeless body in the entrance hall more visible now. His hazel eyes stared first at her then down at his patient, his tall, muscular body slumped in resignation, the rhythmic massage stilling. But his fingers were still knotted together over Gerard's chest as he stared at the monitor.

'There's no history?' he checked. 'Any pre-existing—?'

'He's a workaholic,' Madison whispered. 'That's all I know.'

And the agony she had briefly witnessed was smothered now as Guy reverted to the practical, drew on his professionalism. He flicked on his torch, tested Gerard's pupil response, pulled out his stethoscope and listened for any indication of life, shaking his head as the paramedics rushed in pumped for action, ready to assist. They visibly deflated as they realised who the patient was—anyone who had been in Emergency for any length of time knew and respected Gerard Dalton.

'Time of death.' Guy Boyd's voice was hollow, a muscle flickering in his taut cheek as he glance up at the clock. 'Five thirty-two a.m.'

And Madison did what was needed but no more— she closed Gerard's eyes on a world he had left too soon, pulled a sheet up over his body but not over his face, then walked out of the area, dragging in air that seemed stale, nausea seeping into every pore, nerves jumping as Guy Boyd came up behind her.

'What happened? Before I arrived, I mean.'

'You saw what happened,' Madison choked. 'One minute we were talking, looking forward to today and the next…' She took a deep breath, swallowing rising hysteria. 'His wife, I'll have to—'

'I'll do it,' Guy broke in, but Madison shook her head.

'She deserves more than a phone call.'

'I'll go over to her home now.' He gave a hesitant nod, then midway it changed and he nodded more firmly. 'The hospital doesn't officially open for a few hours yet. I'll go and fetch her.'

'But Yvonne should hear it from someone who knows her…' Tears were starting, emotion was creeping in, but Madison choked it all back, appalled at the prospect of breaking down, terrified that if she started to cry she'd never stop, painfully aware that staff would be arriving soon.

'I know Yvonne,' Guy said, his hand reaching out and capturing her shoulder, squeezing it. Madison couldn't be sure if he was giving support or taking it. 'I'll tell her what's happened face to face—it's better that way. No doubt she'll want to come straight over to the hospital, she'll need to see for herself… Are you OK?' His voice changed from pensive to worried, his hand tightened on her shoulder, but more in an attempt to hold her up. 'Sister…?'

'Madison,' she filled in, running a tongue over horribly dry lips. A scream built in her throat but she swallowed it back, balled her fists, struggled to keep it all in check as blindly Guy continued.

'Madison Walsh,' Guy responded, obviously having recognised her name. 'Gerard speaks very highly of you.' A flash of pain flickered across his face and mercifully he didn't correct himself, didn't relegate Gerard to the past tense while he was still warm in the room nearby. Instead, Guy gulped in air, raked a hand through his hair and then nodded as if to right himself.

'I'll go and tell Yvonne now. This is going to have to go to the coroner, so don't remove any equipment from the…' He gave a tiny swallow before continuing. 'Just make him look as presentable as you can.'

'Of course I will,' Madison snapped, not sure where her anger was coming from, not sure at all how she was actually feeling, but relieved to let a little bit of emotion out. 'As if I need to be told how to prepare a patient.'

'I'm sorry,' Guy said. 'I wasn't implying…' His voice trailed off and Madison stood there trying to take it all in, trying to fathom how somehow in a matter of minutes everything, everything, had changed. 'I'm sorry,' he said again, and Madison knew he wasn't apologising for his words this time but for the terrible loss that had been suffered.

'Me, too,' Madison whispered, wondering how she was going to do this, how she was going to tell the staff. Face Yvonne. Her mind grasped for some comfort, for strength to see her through just the next moment at least. She found it from an unlikely source. Guy Boyd's hand reached for her shoulder, gripping it tightly for a moment in a tender show of support.

'We'll get through this, the department is going to get through this.'

But Madison knew that, knew the team she and Gerard had created, the procedures that had long since been put in place, were enough to withstand even a blow such as this. Her grief was on a much more personal level and when she didn't respond, Guy seemed to sense why.

'He was more than just a boss to you, wasn't he?'

'Much more,' Madison agreed, and perhaps it was the emotion of the moment, a need to voice what was on her mind. Whatever the reason, she found herself opening up in a way she hadn't in the longest time, and even though there were endless things to be addressed, endless problems to face, the two of them took a small slice of time to share in some memories before they faced the unenviable tasks ahead. 'He delivered my daughter.'

'Don't tell me you delivered the baby at work!' Guy teased, but his voice was tinged with something he couldn't identify—regret, confusion, he didn't know. It was hard to believe that this brittle, almost hostile woman should have a softer side, that behind the starched uniform and withering stare beat the infinitely gentler dimensions of a woman.

'Not quite.' A tiny smile wobbled on her lips as

she recalled the memory. 'We needed the money so I worked far into my pregnancy. I was thirty-five weeks pregnant and thought I had a bit of back pain. I tried not to let anyone see, but Gerard, being Gerard, picked up on it straight away. He wanted me to go to Maternity but I insisted on going home first. Being the gentleman he was, he offered to drive me home.'

'You didn't have it in his car!'

Looking up, she saw that hazel eyes were somehow, despite what had happened, smiling.

'No, but I found out what those little handrails above windows are for.' His quizzical frown told Madison that clearly Guy didn't have a clue—no doubt, he thought that they'd merely been provided to hang his dry cleaning from. 'Suddenly I was holding onto the handles, gripping for dear life and wanting to push! Gerard was great. He executed a U-turn in the middle of the road and drove me to Maternity. We made it with seconds to spare.' Like a balloon bursting, the blissful warmth of the memory dispersed and cold reality settled in. 'He was there for me during good times and bad, there for me when my life fell apart…' She checked herself, appalled at admitting so much to a stranger, consoling herself that grief did the strangest things to even the most sensible people. Pressing her fingers into her eyes, Madison halted herself and drew on some extremely well-used inner reserve as Guy watched.

He watched and tried to fathom this woman falling apart—stared down at the very straight brown hair pulled sharply back, the minimal but carefully applied make-up, the crisply ironed burgundy blouse that told everyone she was a senior member of staff, her very neat navy skirt sitting just on the knee and above even neater navy stockinged legs. He wondered what scale she measured herself on because from where he was standing, the closest a woman like Madison Walsh would come to falling apart was a run in her stockings. And no doubt she's have a replacement pair in her bag, and a couple in her office drawer, too, come to that.

'I can't somehow imagine your life falling apart,' he murmured, and Madison let out a hollow laugh.

'Believe me, it did, and through it all Gerard was there.' Feeling horribly self-indulgent, she shot a shy look at Guy. 'From what Gerard told me, you know each other pretty well.'

'Not well enough, unfortunately,' Guy said softly, and there was something in his voice she couldn't interpret, a pain that however well hidden seemed incredibly raw. 'I was hoping to put that right, though. I was really looking forward to working alongside him. I'll go and tell Yvonne,' Guy said wearily, and headed off to perform the hardest task of the entire morning.

CHAPTER TWO

MADISON was glad to be busy and to be able to immerse herself in the seemingly insurmountable task of creating some sort of order out of the chaotic day. When a patient died the work didn't stop. There were relatives to be contacted, forms to be filled out, the body to be prepared. But when the death was sudden, when the patient was also the director of the ward, the workload tripled and Madison dived straight in, discussing the options with Shirley.

'I've paged Terrence Hall, the CEO,' Shirley said crisply, bustling out of Madison's office over to the nurses' station. And though Shirley's voice and actions were supremely efficient, her red-rimmed eyes revealed the inner pain of dealing with the practicalities. 'And I've asked Vic to send all the arriving staff into the main waiting room for a team meeting. I thought it might be easier if we tell everyone at once.'

'That's a good idea,' Madison agreed. 'A lot of the staff will only have met him during orientation or at their interviews, but for those that have worked with him…' She let out a long sigh. 'There are going to be some very upset staff members.'

'How far away does Mrs Dalton live?' Shirley asked, glancing down at her watch and then frowning. 'And will this new consultant know where to go?'

'I expect so—from what Gerard told me, they knew each other well. He didn't ask for an address or directions or anything and, given that it's five minutes or so away, we ought to get things ready.'

By 'things' Madison meant the body, but some words didn't need to be said and both women headed into Resus, determined to do their best for Gerard. And that now meant looking after his family.

Because Gerard's death would most likely have to be investigated by the coroner, all the equipment such as chest pads and IV access had to be left untouched, so Shirley busied herself clearing away the chaos of wrappers and ampoules and syringes, tidying up the area to make it look as presentable as possible. Madison did up Gerard's shirt over the equipment, her shaking hands trying to rearrange his cut tie, placing a pillow under his head and moving his arms out over the sheet so that his family would be able to hold his hands.

'He looks peaceful,' Shirley said, and even though it was a cliché, it was true—in death he looked ten years younger, the tension that must have held him together gone for ever now. 'Should we move him over to a cubicle to give his family more privacy?' She stopped as Guy's solemn face appeared at the curtain. After a brief nod from Madison, he ushered in Gerard's wife and all the words Madison usually delivered at times like these faded before they even formed on her lips. Seeing the usually immaculate, proud Yvonne Dalton's ashen, overwhelmed face as Guy gently guided her in told Madison no words were needed now, that Yvonne only needed to be with her husband.

The guttural scream was heart-wrenching and Madison drew her breath in sharply, biting down on her bottom lip as she guided Yvonne's trembling hand to her husband's while Guy placed a chair behind her, his strong hands helping her to sit.

'Would you like us to leave you alone, Yvonne?' Madison asked. The woman gave a distracted nod.

'Yvonne?' Guy's voice was supremely gentle. 'Can I—?'

'I'm fine.' Yvonne bristled, angry accusing eyes swinging towards him. 'I'd like to be left alone.'

'How was she?' Madison asked when they were out of earshot at the nurses' station. 'When you were at the house?'

'Much as you'd expect,' Guy said, revealing nothing. But his strained expression told Madison it hadn't been easy. 'I rang her son and daughter for her—her hands were shaking too much—and they're on their way in from the City. They shouldn't be very long. Look, I hate to ask, I'm not usually known for passing the buck, but could I ask you to deal with Yvonne when she comes out? I think I'm only upsetting her more.'

'Of course,' Madison agreed, but, seeing his troubled expression, she felt it wasn't quite enough. 'Guy,

I know Yvonne seemed hostile in there but she doesn't blame you for any of this, she's just upset and confused at the moment. You're the one who told her the bad news, so it's you she's reacting to.'

'Perhaps,' Guy said, but he sounded far from convinced. 'But I think it would be better for everyone if I stay in the background while Yvonne's around. OK, bring me up to speed. What have you done while I was gone?'

And even though Madison appreciated the directness of his question, was more than happy to concentrate on practicalities at the moment, she couldn't help but feel Guy was changing the subject. 'Vic's directing all the staff into the main waiting room so that they can be told together. I've got out the interim death certificate forms for you and I've pinned the coroner's number to the front. Shirley—the nurse supervisor—has paged the CEO. I suppose I should let Ambulance Control know.'

'Ambulance Control?' Guy frowned. 'I thought we weren't open to ambulances till eleven.'

'We're not,' Madison said, 'but we can hardly go ahead with opening.' She registered his bemused expression and it infuriated her. 'Guy, I don't think you understand just how pivotal Gerard really is to this department.'

'Perhaps not,' Guy responded, 'but, then, neither do the patients. In fact, I can guarantee that when someone's baby starts convulsing or their husband develops chest pain, the last thing they'll be expecting is a closed-for-business sign on the door. The only thing that will be on their minds is that the new hospital opens to-day—thank heaven help's close at hand.

'We'll address the staff in ten minutes.'

He didn't await her response, which was just as well, Madison realized, because she didn't have one. Instead, he turned and headed off. Seeing Yvonne come out shakily from behind the curtain, Madison guided the distraught woman to the interview room and sat with her in silence for a few minutes as Yvonne quietly wept. She offered the occasional tissue but deliberately didn't speak, allowing Yvonne to guide her in what she needed from Madison.

'When he collapsed…' Yvonne gulped, pleating the tissue between her fingers, her usually strong voice strangled in pain as she forced the words out. 'When Guy arrived and Gerard collapsed, what did he say?'

'He didn't say anything, Yvonne,' Madison said gently. 'It all happened very quickly.'

'I know that,' Yvonne answered through gritted teeth, 'but I need to know what was said, I need to know what—' Her frustrated words halted abruptly and Madison didn't rush to fill the silence, rehearsing in her mind what to say. Yvonne's response was very normal, trying to glean anything she could from the last moments of her loved one's life, trying to find out if something, anything, had been said that she could cling to, a tiny message that maybe she alone might understand. But in Gerard's case there had been nothing and gently Madison attempted to explain that.

'Guy arrived,' Madison said slowly, 'but he was

locked out. Gerard and I were on our way to meet him at Reception. We were just chatting about the day ahead, having a coffee before we started work. Gerard wasn't in pain or anything, I had no idea what was about to happen.' She watched Yvonne frown as she delivered the words and Madison knew that she had to be very gentle, that this short but vital conversation would stay with Yvonne for ever, that she needed to know every detail of her husband's last moments. 'I headed off to let the new consultant in and I thought Gerard was following me, only when I turned around I realized that he was in trouble, he had lost consciousness and was sliding to the floor. He didn't cry out, he didn't complain of any pain. I don't think that Gerard suffered for even a second.'

'And he never regained consciousness?' Yvonne asked, frowning as Madison's words sank in.

'I'm sorry, no,' Madison affirmed. 'I started cardiac massage. Guy had seen what had happened and raced around to assist. He grabbed some vital equipment on the way and we both did everything we could to save your husband, but unfortunately there was nothing that could be done.'

'He didn't say anything?' Yvonne checked. 'He didn't speak to Guy?'

'No.'

'I don't believe you,' Yvonne snapped, her eyes angry now. 'I need to know what was said, Madison!'

Madison now frowned, uncertain what Yvonne wanted to know. Initially she had assumed Yvonne was hoping for some tiny whisper from Gerard, a deathbed declaration, but as Madison stared back at the other woman she wasn't sure what, if anything, Yvonne was hoping to hear. Checking herself, Madison forced the muscles in her face to relax, to wipe away her slightly perturbed frown, and, as she had learnt in counseling sessions with bereaved relatives, to let Yvonne lead the way.

'You're telling me,' Yvonne finally continued when Madison remained silent, 'that Gerard collapsed and died without a single word, that there was no exchange of words between him and you or Guy?'

'None,' Madison confirmed. 'Yvonne, I wish I could say different, I wish that Gerard had had enough time to say what he wanted to, but the truth is he didn't. I know at the moment that doesn't give you much comfort, but in the days and weeks that follow maybe you'll be able to draw some strength from the fact that Gerard truly didn't suffer, that not for a single moment was he anything other than the vibrant man we all knew and loved.'

'I do.' Yvonne nodded. 'You're right, Madison, I take a lot of comfort from that.'

Madison watched as Yvonne visibly relaxed, watched as her words sank in. She was slightly taken aback to see just how quickly those words appeared to take effect.

'Thank you for your help, Madison, and for all you did for Gerard. Now, if you'll excuse me, I'd like to make a few telephone calls. Could I trouble someone for a cup of coffee?'

'Of course.' Madison nodded. 'I'll arrange for a tray to be brought in to you.'

'And would it be possible to have some headache tablets? I don't have any in my bag.'

'I'll get you some now.'

Slightly bemused by Yvonne's rather abrupt turn-around, Madison quietly left the room, closing the door gently behind her. She frowned as she did so, then gave herself a quick mental shake. It wasn't for her to judge—she'd dealt with literally hundreds of bereaved relatives in her time and if she'd learnt one thing, it was that no two reactions were the same.

People grieved in their own way.

By the time Madison had given Yvonne two head-ache tablets and asked Vic if he would mind making Mrs Dalton a cup of coffee, preferably in a china cup if he could find one, her ten minutes were more than up. Grimacing as she glanced at her watch, she headed off to the waiting room, finally ready to address the staff and let them know what had taken place and the reason they had been ushered in for this impromptu meeting. It never entered her head that Guy would have already started, that by the time she arrived at the waiting-room entrance the news would already have been broken!

'This has come as a huge shock to all of us, espe-cially to those of you who have had the pleasure of working alongside Gerard over the years. However…' He paused just long enough for the shocked chatter to stop, just long enough to shift the tone and command the room. 'We have a department due to open in less than two hours and ambulances will be pulling into the bay in less than four, and that means I need some honesty from you guys. I need you to decide honestly whether or not you're able to work. If not, go home.'

The brutality of his words had Madison inwardly wincing. She fought an impulse to walk right up and override him—how dared he swan in and demand peak efficiency? How dared he act as if nothing had really happened! But as Guy continued talking, she found herself listening instead, examining her own conscience as he eloquently continued.

'There can be no excuses,' Guy explained. 'If you can't do your job today then you're welcome to leave with no further explanation. I'll sign you off on compassionate leave with full pay. I don't want to be staring at a pile of incident reports at the end of the day, I don't want to hear that you were so upset about what happened that you gave the wrong drug or made an error of judgement, I don't want to sit in the interview room with grieving relatives, knowing that their loved one didn't receive the best possible care. Now, have a coffee and try to get your head around what's happened, and then, those who are up for it, business as usual in fifteen minutes.' For the first time in his speech his eyes met Madison's. 'Gerard Dalton wouldn't expect anything less from any of you.'

'He's good, isn't he?' Shirley whispered. 'Personally, I was all ready to close the department for the day, but what Guy says makes sense, doesn't it?'

'I guess.' Madison shrugged, but her shoulders were

so rigid with tension they barely moved. She watched as the staff swarmed around Guy, asking questions, seeking reassurance, turning to him. She hated herself for being so petty.

Guy had achieved in minutes what had taken her months to achieve.

He'd created a team.

As the crowd dispersed, Guy made his way over. 'Well?' Pretending she had no idea what he was talking about, Madison frowned up at him.

'Well, what?'

'Are you staying or going home?'

'It was never my intention to go home,' Madison responded through slightly gritted teeth. 'I merely suggested that we delay opening the department for a day. However, on reflection, I can see it would be better to go ahead as planned.'

'Good,' Guy responded, and Madison couldn't help feeling as if he'd won a battle she hadn't even realised had been taking place.

'Right!' She gave a brisk smile. 'I'd better go and check on Yvonne, and, given that the staff are all here and we'll be opening shortly, you'll be wanting to get changed.'

'Changed?' It was Guy frowning now.

'You are the new consultant?' Madison pretended to check, running a slightly dismissive eye over his jeans and T-shirt.

'Oh.' Guy let out relieved laugh and started to rummage in his pocket. Madison watched in horror as he pulled out an ID badge and hung it around his neck. 'Thanks for reminding me!'

'So how was your first day?' Helen beamed, pulling open her front door and ushering Madison inside. 'You must be exhausted.'

'I am,' Madison agreed, nodding gratefully as Helen held up the kettle. She collapsed into a chair at the kitchen table. 'How was Emily?'

'Great,' Helen answered brightly. 'She didn't miss you for a second! So? Don't keep me in suspense—was it busy, any dramas on the first day?'

Madison was saved from answering by noisy five-year-old footsteps running in from the garden where Emily had been playing with Helen's son. And with her first genuine smile for the last twelve hours lighting up her face, Madison scooped Emily up and hugged her fiercely for a moment.

'Did you have a good day at school?' A vague nod was Madison's only answer, but from the bright stains all over her dress, clearly she'd been painting. 'And how about last night, were you good for Helen?' A tiny guilty glance in Helen's direction was followed by a beat of a pause. 'Richard and me were talking until late, and Helen had to tell us to be quiet.'

'Richard and I,' Madison corrected, but Emily just frowned.

'No, it was Richard and me who were talking.'

'Well, next time you go to sleep when Helen tells

you,' Madison lightly scolded, smothering a smile at Emily's response.

'So how was your day?' Emily asked. Her pretty rosebud mouth deftly changed the subject and for the first of a hundred times in any one day Madison could see Mark, Emily's father, etched in every feature, from her winning smile and stunning looks right down to her ability to shift a subject from anything remotely serious. 'Did anyone die?' Emily asked, with all the tact of a five-year-old. 'Did you look after any kids that were sick? Was the vending machine filled up in time for the hospital opening?'

'Yes, yes, and yes,' Madison answered, grateful that the only answer Emily was really interested in was the last one. The emergency waiting room's vending machines held an in inordinate amount of fascination for Emily and many evenings were spent asking exactly how the empty racks were going to be filled, how the special 'lady' who stocked it when the waiting room was quiet was going to get her hand up through the tiny space at the bottom and fill all the slots. Madison hadn't actually had the heart to tell her daughter that the 'lady' actually had a key that opened the glass door!

'Here,' Madison said, pulling two chocolate bars out of her bag, uncharacteristically not asking Helen if it was too close to dinner for Richard to have a treat. 'I got you these from the vending machine. As it turns out, you were the first customer. Go and give one of these to Richard and play for ten minutes. I'll call you in soon.'

'What happened today?' Helen asked as Emily scampered off, her voice filled with concern.

'How do you know anything happened?'

'Well, it's the first time in living memory you've given the kids chocolate so close to dinner, and the first time you haven't pulled out Emily's homework diary to check that it had been filled in.'

'Am I that predictable?' Madison sighed.

'Wonderfully so.' Helen grinned, placing a steaming mug of coffee in front of Madison and waiting till she took a long grateful sip before resuming the conversation. 'So what went down today?'

'Gerard Dalton collapsed and died.'

There had been no easy way to say it, so Madison had just gone right ahead, nodding grimly at Helen's shocked expression to confirm the terrible news. 'We'd both arrived at work, there was no one else in the department and we were going over the day's plans. He'd just made me a coffee...' She gave a tiny ghost of a smile as Helen, with a rather startled look, promptly put down her own mug. 'Sudden death isn't catching, Helen!'

'Sorry,' Helen mumbled. 'Go on.'

'So, it was just the two of us in the department, the new consultant had arrived, but the emergency doors were closed and he was locked outside. We were going around to meet him when I realised Gerard wasn't walking with me. I turned around and he'd collapsed.'

'Did he say he had chest pain?' Helen asked, clearly

stunned but her medical brain trying to fathom out what had happened.

'He said nothing.' Madison blinked into her coffee. 'Nothing. One minute we were chatting, and I headed off to go and the next I turned around and he was sliding onto the floor. Looking back on things, I think Gerard was actually dead before he hit the ground. He didn't stand a chance.'

'So what caused it?'

'We don't know yet.' Madison gave an exasperated shrug. 'There'll be an autopsy, of course, but for now it could be anything—cerebral, cardiac or a PE maybe. For a moment there it looked as if it could be a ruptured aneurysm—he'd been complaining of mild back pain but as I pointed out, he'd strained his back lifting a box the night before.'

'You'd get a bit more warning with an aneurysm, you'd think,' Helen pondered out loud. As a surgical nurse she'd seen her fair share. 'I mean, he'd have been pale and sweaty, in some sort of distress.'

'He was nothing like that,' Madison said. 'Given it's Gerard, I'm sure the autopsy will take place very quickly and I'd expect we'd have some answers by tomorrow. Not that it's going to help. You should have seen his poor wife and children, they were absolutely devastated. It came completely out of the blue. They're such a close family.'

'And you were there on your own?' Helen gasped.

'Only for a couple of moments,' Madison corrected. 'Like I said, the new consultant had arrived and even though he couldn't get in straight away, he saw what was happening through the glass doors and raced around.'

'Poor thing,' Helen sighed. Madison was grateful for the coffee and sympathy, glad to peel off her shoes for five minutes and dunk a chocolate biscuit in her coffee. But when Helen continued talking, with a jolt Madison realised her sympathy hadn't been aimed towards her. 'It must have been awful for him. Imagine that happening on your first day!'

'He seemed to deal with it all OK.' Madison chewed her lip as she thought back over the day. 'He just got on with it, I guess.'

'Only because he had no choice,' Helen pointed out. 'Imagine starting a new job and your mentor and senior dropping dead. Poor thing, I bet it was all left for him to carry.'

'Not all of it,' Madison answered, but her response was a touch too quick, just a tad too defensive. As busy and as awful as her own day had been, for Guy it must have been far worse. Despite the fact the hospital was brand-new, they'd had a generous number of patients and Guy, with no senior on hand and no orientation day behind him, had had to deal with the lot. From critically ill patients to just the basics everyone encountered when they started a new job—such as where the loo was located, the coffee-mugs, the X-ray pads. It was the first time Madison had actually thought about it, the first time she had really taken stock and looked at the events from someone else's perspective. A wave of guilt washed over her.

Throughout the day, Guy had repeatedly asked her how she was bearing up, had even made her a cup of tea and bought her a sandwich from the machine at around two when he'd realised that she hadn't eaten. And what had she done for him?

Precisely nothing!

'Gosh.' Helen blinked. 'What a terrible start.'

'It was.' Madison grimaced. 'I'm going to try and not think about it, at least until I've got Emily into bed.'

'Good idea,' Helen agreed sympathetically. 'Switch that brain off for a couple of hours—it must have been an exhausting day. Do you want to stay here for dinner?'

Madison was about to say no, to shake her head and call for Emily to collect her things, but the prospect of going home, of pulling one of many frozen casseroles out of the freezer and attempting to be normal after the day she'd had, had Madison changing her shake to a nod.

'That would be great, if you're sure you don't mind.'

'Mind? Life's so much easier when Richard's got someone to play with. And, before you ask, despite Emily's guilty look, she was actually a delight last night. They were both asleep by eight.'

'Good.' Madison gave a relieved smile, then chewed her lip nervously, taking a deep breath before continuing. 'Helen? Given what's happened today, I actually can't see me managing to get away on time for a while.' Madison gave a guilty shuffle in her seat, which Helen easily interpreted.

'Don't worry if you're late home over the next couple of weeks, it doesn't matter a scrap. You were always going to be busy, with the department opening, and with what's just happened you can hardly be expected to just walk out at three-thirty!'

'You don't mind?' Madison checked, relief flooding her.

They had an arrangement with childcare that only two women could have engineered or understood. Both were single parents, both lived in the same street, both were nurses, which meant guilt heaped upon guilt, trying to juggle work and motherhood. Two years ago, moaning over their questionable cappuccinos, courtesy of the canteen's new machine, they had come to a tentative agreement. Madison dropped Emily off at seven each morning, leaving Helen to give her breakfast and do the school run, as well as picking Emily up from school. Madison's shifts normally finished at three-thirty but as a NUM her work hours were as close to nine to five as nursing got, and even when she'd worked at her old hospital, which was further away, more often than not Madison's car had pulled into Helen's drive only a moment or two after Helen's. But it was great to know that Emily was taken care of and not to have to rush away from work if the situation dictated that she stay. In return for Helen doing the school run, Madison had Richard to sleep over one night a week to enable Helen to do a night shift—or a 'sanity shift', as Helen called it.

And two years in, despite Madison moving to the new hospital, despite the occasional hiccup when one of them was sick, somehow the system they had created that long-ago morning still stood strong.

'I don't a mind a bit if you're late for a couple of weeks,' Helen carried, her voice a touch higher as she asked for a favour of her own. 'Actually, it will make me feel less guilty, asking you for a favour! I need a babysitter on Friday night.'

'Are you doing an extra "sanity shift"?' Madison grinned. 'Sure, no problem. I'd be happy to have him. We can both be guilt-free about dumping on each other.'

'Not me, I'm afraid. Guilt's going to be my best friend for the next few days.' Helen winced, then, screwing her eyes closed, she blurted out the last four words Madison had expected to hear.

'I've got a date!'

'Oh!' Madison blinked. 'With a man?'

'No,' Helen answered, with her tongue firmly in her cheek. 'With a hot-looking lesbian I met. Of course with a man!'

'I'm sorry.' Madison gave an embarrassed laugh. 'I had no idea you were seeing anyone.'

'I'm not—at least not yet. It's our first date and if I ask Mum to babysit she's going to read a million and one things into it. It's just easier not to say anything at this stage.'

'So, what's he like?' Madison asked. 'How did you meet him?'

'At the school playground, of all places.' Helen giggled. 'He's a single dad. He just moved to the area. His wife died. Ages ago,' Helen added hastily. 'So he's got no baggage.'

'My husband died ages ago,' Madison reminded her, 'and I'm still paying excess.'

'But you're so-o complicated,' Helen teased.

'If you're over thirty, you've got baggage,' Madison said dryly. 'So, does this single dad with zero baggage have a name?'

'Matthew.'

'A job?'

'He's a carpenter.'

'How many kids?'

'One.' Helen gave a tiny shudder. 'Thank God. Imagine if he had triplets?'

'Perish the thought,' Madison said, pulling a face. 'So where's your man taking you?'

'I don't know.' Helen beamed. 'He just said to wear smart-casual.'

'Which could mean anything,' Madison warned. 'You should have seen what Guy turned up in today. Jeans, sneakers and a T-shirt. And when I told him to get changed, all he did was put on a name badge.' To her utter indignation Helen started to laugh. 'It's not funny,' Madison snapped.

'Oh, but it is.' Helen giggled. 'Given what a stickler you are for uniforms!'

'I am not,' Madison replied hotly. 'I just like to look smart.' Helen raised a very knowing eyebrow, which Madison badly wanted to ignore but found she couldn't. 'It makes the patients feel more secure to see a well-presented staff member. A doctor rocking up to the bedside in jeans hardly inspires confidence.'

'Well, if I were a patient, I wouldn't give a damn what the doctor was wearing,' Helen mused. 'So long as he knew what he was doing and could actually manage to look me in the eye and talk to me on occasions. There are plenty of doctors in thousand-dollar suits with the most appalling bedside manner.'

'Perhaps,' Madison reluctantly conceded.

'Is he good-looking?' Helen asked, and Madison wished she hadn't. In fact, she dearly wanted this conversation to be over.

'I guess,' Madison answered tartly. 'If you like the "just got out of bed and bypassed the shower" look.'

'Oh, but I do.' Helen giggled. 'Is he single?'

'I didn't ask.' Madison bristled. 'But from what Gerard told me, I'd assume so. He's completely irresponsible—apparently he'd only commit to six months with the department.'

'Hardly a hanging offence,' Helen said laughingly, but Madison didn't join in.

'Gerard told me that when he appointed him, Guy had spent most of his medical career travelling the world, gaining experience. Which is fine and everything, but it hardly paints him as the most reliable of men!'

'He must be rich, though, if he can afford to turn down a decent job.'

'Money isn't everything,' Madison said tartly.

'He sounds perfectly lovely,' Helen sighed. 'Maybe we can double date.'

'I'm fully booked this century,' Madison snapped. And given Helen wasn't going to move, she made herself busy, slicing cucumber for the salad and putting on a pan of water for the rice. Even though the conversation had ended a good couple of minutes ago, Madison found herself reviving it. 'Believe me, Guy Boyd would be the last person I'd date.'

'Perhaps.' Helen smiled, not rising to Madison's rather brittle tone. 'But have you ever thought of getting back out there?'

'Out where?' Madison asked, knowing perfectly well what Helen meant but deliberately stalling her.

'Dating, Madison,' Helen said. 'It's been five years since Mark died…'

'And it's taken me nearly all of them to get back on my feet,' Madison pointed out. 'I used the words "free spirit" affectionately when I first met Mark,' Madison said. 'I thought it was fun to follow your heart, live for today. I really believed Mark when he said that tomorrow would take care of itself. But unlike Mark, having a baby made me grow up, having a baby meant that I did start thinking about tomorrow…'

'Madison, I know you've been hurt…' Standing up, Helen checked the door was closed. 'Heaven knows, you've got every reason to be wary, but there are some good guys out there.'

'How do you know that?' Madison's words were as confused as they were angry. 'I'm doing OK. Emily and I are doing just fine by ourselves!' She shook her head, not at all ready to go there after such an emotionally charged day. 'Can we drop it?'

'Sure,' Helen said kindly, but her tiny sigh told Madison that she'd have loved to have carried on with the conversation, would have loved to have pushed a little more. After a moment's hesitation, a moment to wait and see if Madison was going to add anything further, Helen gave in and headed over to the fridge. She pulled out some chicken, chatting about something Richard had said to Emily. But as grateful as Madison was for the change of subject, inside she felt jolted and uneasy, and it wasn't just to do with Gerard's death but with the pace of her own life. The fact that Helen, after the appalling marriage she'd been through, after swearing off men for the next century at least, could even contemplate taking up the baton and resuming the race was beyond Madison's comprehension.

Helen was moving on with her life, suggesting even that Madison do the same.

Only she truly wasn't ready.

CHAPTER THREE

'IT'S sports uniform today!' Emily said accusingly as she eyed her uniform, crisply laid out on the sofa.

'Which is what I've put out for you,' Madison answered, depositing a glass of fruit juice on the coffee-table for her daughter. She started applying her foundation as she made a speedy exit towards the bathroom.

'You gave me stripy socks!' Emily's words stopped Madison in her tracks, her un-mascara'd eyelashes blinking at the simple but unusual mistake. 'They have to be plain white socks, but these have got a red stripe around the top!'

'Then I'll get you some plain white ones,' Madison answered, annoyed at herself for that simple slip-up. The morning routine was usually written in stone, but the morning wasn't normally preceded by a fitful night spent tossing and turning. To Madison's shame, it hadn't just been Gerard's sudden death that had kept her staring at the ceiling into the small hours, but Helen's rather pointed comments. Despite the irrefutable evidence, Madison resisted the thought—was it the very new, very inappropriate consultant who had caused her sudden brush with insomnia?

He unsettled her.

Heading into Emily's bedroom on autopilot, she opened the top drawer in the chest and pulled out a pair of neatly folded white socks without even having to look. But she did. She stood and looked, with her fingers still massaging the foundation into her cheek, at the rows of neatly folded white socks, the perfectly ironed knickers. Her eyes then darted around the room, taking in the neatly ordered bookshelves, the already made bed, and, instead of drawing comfort from it, it unnerved her.

'Here!' Madison said, handing Emily the socks, wondering, not for the first time either, what other five-year-old would even have noticed a single red stripe.

Wondering, not for the first time, if maybe, just maybe, Helen was right and it was time to loosen up a touch.

Back in the bathroom Madison stared at her reflection in the mirror, taking in the neutral foundation, no doubt to be accentuated by the neutral blusher and lipstick that was about to follow—years' worth of order and restraint summed up in her make-up bag.

And for what?

'Morning, Madison!' A cheerful wave from Max, a paramedic, coupled with a roll of his eyes told Madison that he wasn't overly concerned with the condition of the patient on the stretcher. Glancing at the large grimacing face of the woman, clutching her stomach and writhing in pain, Madison immediately understood why. 'Is there anyone I can hand this patient over to?'

'Won't I do?'

'You're the NUM.' Max grinned. 'Shouldn't you be in your office?'

He was joking, sort of. As an NUM, the department was her responsibility and it didn't allow much time for patient contact—unless there was a complaint to deal with! And patient contact was something Madison sorely missed.

'Sorry.' Alanna, one of the RNs, dashed over. 'I've got this, Madison. I was just taking a patient up to the ward. You can go back to whatever you were doing.'

And even though she undoubtedly meant it with the best intentions, inwardly Madison bristled. Alanna had actually gone for the NUM position as well, and even though she had insisted there were no hard feelings when Madison had been given the job, Madison wasn't entirely convinced that was the case. Alanna wanted to be filling Madison's shoes, but perversely sometimes Madison wanted to be wearing Alanna's. Holding on firmly to the casualty card, Madison forced a smile. 'I'll take this patient. Why don't you go and have your coffee-break, Alanna?'

It came as no surprise when her smile wasn't returned.

'We got the call as a Julie Bartram, collapsed at the petrol station,' Max said. 'However, when we arrived we found it to actually be Judith Baker, forty-eight years old, with a past history of multiple abdominal operations and—'

'I know Judith's history.' Madison gave a slightly wry smile. Practically every emergency department in the state of Victoria knew Judith's history, along with a few interstate hospitals she had frequented. Judith had a rare and complicated disease that went by the rather grand name of Munchausen's syndrome, a baffling and extremely frustrating condition whereby the patient invented dramatic symptoms in an effort to get themselves admitted to hospital, often enduring unnecessary and painful procedures. And Judith had endured plenty. Listed in most emergency rooms, she often went under different names, but invariably she would be recognised or her story would alert the staff that this wasn't a genuine patient and after a few enquiries the truth would come out...

'I'm really sick, Sister,' Judith gasped. 'My stomach's killing me. I really mean it this time.'

'Let's get her into cubicle two, guys, please,' Madison directed, but Max gave her a startled look, clearly expecting Judith to be sent, as was more usual, to the waiting room.

'Cubicle two?' Max checked, shrugging when Madison gave a swift nod. She waited till they'd settled Judith on the gurney and then followed them outside when Max beckoned.

'She called for an ambulance three times over the weekend. She's got three bottles of painkillers in her bag, each one under a different name!'

'I don't doubt that she has,' Madison said. 'She's probably been "doctor shopping", Max, but you know that I'm far from a soft touch. I've sent Judith to the waiting room on many occasions, even walked her out of the department myself when I felt she was playing games, but today I don't like the look of her.'

'Fair enough,' Max agreed, then his tone shifted. 'Do you know when the funeral…?'

'Not yet.' Madison responded crisply to the question that everyone was asking today. 'As soon as I hear I'll post a notice in the staffroom and I'll ring the ambulance depot.'

'It's gonna be big,' Max said. 'A lot of people will want to pay their respects. Will you be doing a reading or talking about him?'

'Me?' Madison gave a slightly startled look.

'Well, you've worked with him for ages, you both set up this place…'

'I'm sure there are far more relevant people in Gerard's life to talk about him,' Madison responded, then swiftly changed the subject. 'I'd better get back to Judith.'

'No one believes me,' Judith said as Madison started to undress her. 'They all think I'm putting it on.'

'You understand why they think that, don't you?' Madison replied. 'Judith, you've abused the system so many times, we've had this conversation on numerous occasions—you begging to be believed, insisting that this time there really is something wrong, only to find out a few days or weeks and heaven knows how many tests or operations later that there was, in fact, nothing wrong.'

'You don't believe me.' Judith shivered. 'Look at me. Surely you can tell that this time I'm not pretending?'

But could she? Madison stared down at her patient, at the pale brown hair with grey roots that needed retouching, at the beads of sweat on her forehead. She felt the racing pulse beneath her fingertips and truly didn't know—Judith had come in in the same condition before, on one occasion she had even injected herself with insulin to induce similar symptoms, with near fatal consequences.

Judith knew as much as Madison did about hospitals. More perhaps. She knew how to fake her symptoms, had taken drugs to produce symptoms, had lied over and over again to get to the top of the list, had called more ambulances than Madison had ever called taxis, and though her games had seemed to have stopped for a while, it would seem she was up to her old tricks, giving false identities to unwitting doctors to obtain prescriptions, and calling ambulances at will.

But even though the evidence was stacked against Judith, Madison actually had a lingering fear that, after all this time, Judith's pain could be genuine.

'You've lied today, Judith, and yesterday, too...' Holding up the bottles of medicine Max had handed her, Madison showed them to her patient. 'These drugs have been prescribed from doctors hundreds of kilometres away, so how can you expect me to believe that you're telling the truth?'

'I tried over and over to get seen locally using my own name. I was in agony and no one believed me, so I knew I had to go where they didn't know me.'

'So you got up to your old tricks?' Madison asked, but it was entirely without bitterness. Her brow furrowed as she tried to assess her patient, tried to imagine the desperate measures a woman like Judith would go to to get seen by a doctor.

'I had no choice,' Judith begged. 'I was in agony, my stomach was killing me.' Her voice was rising in hysteria, her hands clutching Madison's, begging her to believe her—again.

'Judith, I'm going to do your observations.' Madison's voice in contrast was calm. She attached Judith to the blood-pressure machine, checked her pulse and temperature, and noted that it was low. But Judith's temperature had been low before, courtesy of a plug of wax in her ear to give an abnormal reading. In the past blood tests had revealed abnormally high levels of caffeine in her system to produce a racing pulse. She'd once even strategically taped stones to her body to give on X-ray the appearance of renal colic. Over and over Judith had abused the system, over and over she'd begged the staff to believe that this time she really meant it, that this time she wasn't crying wolf. And she'd been believed.

'I'm going to get a doctor to see you, Judith, but you need to be honest. You need to say exactly what has happened. Don't try to make things up or exaggerate your symptoms—just tell the truth.'

Stepping out of the cubicle, Madison scanned the department, instantly disregarding two of the more junior doctors. Whether or not Judith was playing games, an experienced doctor was needed, and the only one in view right now was Guy Boyd, who was carefully examining an X-ray of a child's elbow, his long fingers tracing the outline, then turning it around to get a different angle. Even though he was the obvious choice, because of what had happened yesterday Madison didn't want to go to him. She wanted to avoid contact with him as much as possible, embarrassed that she had let down her guard a touch. For some reason he made her feel exposed and vulnerable, and for a woman as in control as Madison, that wasn't something she wanted to feel.

But the patient had to come first and right now Guy was the man for the job.

'Where,' Guy asked dryly as Madison joined him at the viewing box, 'did patients go before this place opened? I can't believe we're full.'

'I was thinking the same,' Madison admitted. 'It's the same with shopping centres.'

'Shopping centres?'

'A new one opens and within a couple of days the lines at the checkout are full, there are people spilling out of cafés. I always wonder where they did their shopping previously.' She was chatting idly while jotting down her own observations about Judith, being very careful to be objective with her findings, to push aside the appalling history of the patient. 'Can you see a patient for me?'

'Actually, I'm seeing five at the moment.' Guy grimaced. 'Is it anything very urgent?'

'I'm not sure,' Madison admitted. Guy turned away from the X-ray he was looking at, hearing the concern in her voice. 'Judith's particularly difficult. She was one of the regulars at my old hospital, and a few more besides.' She held out the card for him to see if he recognised the name but Guy shook his head.

'Unless she's been to a hospital in India recently, I won't recognise her…'

'I wouldn't put it past Judith,' Madison joked weakly.

'Is she a hospital-hopper?'

'One of the best,' Madison said, glad that he had got the drift. 'No doubt the receptionist at my old hospital is having to pull out a wheelbarrow to send over her old notes. She's had multiple operations, numerous admissions, she's made a complete fool of me on more than one occasion and she may be about to again, but…'

'You don't think that she's faking it this time?'

'I don't know,' Madison admitted. 'I just can't judge it with Judith, but I do believe that she's scared, and she's actually admitted that she's lied to get seen over the last few days. I've probably just had the most honest conversation ever with her, but whether this is just an even more elaborate scheme of hers to drag us in, I can't say. I think she needs a senior doctor to look at her.' Madison glanced over at Brad, an exceptionally eager intern. 'She'd wipe the floor with him.' Madison sighed. Looking back, she was slightly startled to see Guy smiling at her observation—not the rather mocking smile he had worn when he'd put his ID badge on yesterday, but a kinder, gentler smile that lit up his eyes, made him, for a moment, look as young as Brad. Madison was startled at the effect it had on her. Guy Boyd embodied everything she avoided in a man.

'Well, then, I'd better take a look,' Guy said, taking the card from Madison. 'Would you mind coming with me? Given that you know her, no doubt you'll realise, sooner than I, if she's up to her tricks.'

'Doctor?' Alanna was back from her coffee-break, blushing furiously as she looked up at Guy, and Madison was sure it had nothing to do with his seniority and everything to do with six feet three of tousled, rugged sex appeal. 'Could you, please, write up a new IV order for cubicle eight? The saline's just about through.'

'Sure,' Guy said easily, taking the card, apparently not noticing Alanna's furious blush. But he was probably used to women being three shades of crimson darker when he was around. In his world, no doubt, it was entirely normal to have women acting like gauche teenagers. The jeans had gone, instead he was dressed today in theatre greens and a pair of sneakers. A stethoscope hung from his neck and a pen was in the V-neck of his top. He pulled out the pen and started writing up the further IV order. His ID badge was clipped to the top pocket and, despite the unflattering lines of the theatre greens, it was evident there was a toned body beneath, a deeply tanned toned body, Madison mentally added, seeing the sun-bleached hairs on his forearms as he filled in the orders and handed the card back to Alanna. 'I'll be in to check on him soon. Can you let the patient know that I haven't forgotten him?'

'Right.' He smiled again at Madison. 'Let's go and say hi to Judith.'

'Good morning, Mrs Baker.' Supremely polite, he entered the cubicle. 'I hear that you have some stomach pain.'

'I have,' Judith sobbed. 'And no one believes me. For the last four days I've been trying to get someone—'

'Forget about that now,' Guy cut in, his voice crisp and commanding. 'Can you tell me when the pain started?'

'On Saturday,' Judith replied. 'I woke up with it.'

'Any vomiting?'

'Lots.'

'OK.' Guy nodded. 'And have you had a fever?' He looked down at the casualty card, which gave Judith's low temperature reading.

'I did, I really did, Doctor. I know it isn't up now but I was shaking and sweating. I took it myself and it was over forty degrees.'

'How did you get to…?' He frowned as he picked up one of the medicine bottles, looking at the name of the chemist that had dispensed the drug.

'Moe,' Judith answered for him. 'I asked a friend to drive me and finally we found a doctor's surgery that had a doctor who would take a look at me, someone who didn't know who I was. I'd tried to be seen by a few of the local doctors but I'm blacklisted.'

'Why's that?' Guy asked, and Madison could only admire him. Even though she had explained the problem to Guy, he was giving Judith the opportunity to tell her own story. She was pleating the sheet beneath her fingers and Madison watched the tears of pain, frustration and utter humiliation rolling down Judith's cheeks.

'Because I make things up.'

'What sort of things?' Guy asked, as if it were the most natural question in the world.

'Illnesses,' Judith sobbed. 'I lie so that I can get myself admitted to hospital.' When Guy didn't say anything and was clearly waiting for more information, finally Judith elaborated. 'I've had hundreds of tests, loads of operations and none of them were needed.'

'How did you do that?' Guy asked. 'Have you had any medical training?'

'No.' Judith shook her head angrily, and for a moment a flash of the old Judith returned, a flash of the manipulative, scheming woman who had graced so many hospital corridors. 'But I can read and, much to the doctors' indignation, I'm actually clever. They hate to think that someone without a medical degree might actually know more than them, hate to think that they've been fooled—'

'I'd hate it, too,' Guy admitted, halting her angry tirade. 'I'd hate to think I'd put anyone, no matter how much they thought they needed it, through a medical procedure that wasn't warranted—when clearly they needed a different kind of help.' He stared directly at her and Madison noted that it was Judith who looked away first. 'You've obviously pretended to have stomach pain before.'

'But I haven't done it for ages,' Judith whispered through chattering teeth.

'Why not?'

'Because I didn't want to live like that any more. I've been seeing a psychiatrist. She's been wonderful, and we've been sorting the mess out.'

'The mess?' Guy asked.

'The mess in my head.' Judith tried to shout, but the pain forced her back on the pillow, sobbing in defeat as she lay there.

'OK, can you show me where the pain is?' Guy asked.

Madison lifted Judith's gown, silently appalled at the numerous scars—a legacy of her disorder.

'It's all over,' Judith gasped as Guy probed her stomach. Taking his stethoscope from around his neck, he listened for a full minute for bowel sounds.

'Have you taken any medication, apart from these?' Guy asked, gesturing to the various painkillers that had been found in her bag.

'Nothing.' Judith shook her head, but Guy just stared, clearly not convinced. 'I took some laxatives. I thought if I could go to the toilet, that might help.'

'OK, let me listen to your chest.' Gently, with Madison's help, he leant her forward and listened to her chest. For fifteen minutes he conducted a full and very thorough examination, before finally replacing the blanket and opening one of the silver trolleys in the cubicle to prepare to put in an IV.

'You won't be able to do it,' Judith said, as Guy applied a tourniquet. 'My veins are all scarred and collapsed because of all the times they've been used.'

'All the unnecessary times,' Guy corrected her, and Judith nodded pitifully.

'Normally they call for an anaesthetist or I have to go to Theatre to have a PICC line put in.'

'Just stay very still,' Guy said quietly. 'I think I've got one.'

He had!

Madison gave a blink of admiration. She knew only too well that Judith's veins were almost impossible to gain access to. Years and years of abuse had rendered this simple procedure practically impossible, yet with one attempt Guy had succeeded.

'Africa.' He gave a small smile and looked up at Madison. 'If you can get a needle into a premature, malnourished, collapsed baby, then you can get one into Judith.'

'Thank you, Doctor.'

'Don't thank me yet.' Guy shook his head. 'Now, Judith, I'm not going to give you anything for pain—' As she opened her mouth to protest Guy got there first. 'It has nothing to do with whether or not I believe you, or punishing you or anything like that at all. The fact is, until we know what's going on, until the surgeons have seen you...'

'They won't look at me,' Judith said. 'I can't take this pain for much longer.'

'I'm going to send you for an urgent CT scan of your abdomen and I'll talk to the surgeons myself. In the meantime, we'll put an NG tube down—that's a small tube that goes from your nose into your stomach and drains…' He gave a small shrug. 'You know what an NG tube is, I'm sure. Now, that might give you some comfort but at the very least it will empty your stomach and stop the nausea. My preliminary diagnosis is an obstruction, probably caused by adhesions.' His voice was very clear and very firm as he spoke to Judith, refusing for even a second to be pulled into one of her mind games. 'After even one operation, there is a chance of adhesions. They're like a spider web of glue in the stomach, and, given the amount of surgery you've had in the past, it's inevitable that there will be a lot of scar tissue and adhesions.'

'So I really am sick this time.'

'I think that you are,' Guy admitted. 'But possibly, looking at your history, you're having me on. I'm telling you, Judith, not as a threat, not trying to be unkind—given the amount of surgery you've had in the past, you are going to have a lot of very real health problems in the future with just this type of thing, and you're going to need serious medical help. So if you're playing games today, stop it now, tell me now and at least we'll both know where we stand, because if this is just a need to get admitted to hospital, if this is attention-seeking behaviour, it has to stop right here and now, before I go out on a limb for you.'

Madison watched as he gave Judith a chance to come clean, a chance to back down. Despite Judith's poor track record, so emphatic were Guy's words, so utterly direct and to the point, Madison felt that if Judith was lying, if she was playing one of her elaborate games, then Guy had said enough to convince her to stop it right there and then.

'It isn't.'

'OK,' Guy said. 'I actually do believe you, Judith. But if I'm proved wrong, next time I'm not going to be so ready to be convinced.'

'I know that, Doctor.'

'OK.' He gave a small nod. 'I'll get this blood to the lab and arrange some tests, and I'll also talk to the surgeons. And I'm going to get Madison to apply a shield to the IV keypad and lock it.'

'I'm not going to change the dosage,' Judith said.

'No doubt you have in the past, though. Judith, I'm going to be completely frank with you and that starts here. I am going to remove the IV trolley so that you can't take anything, I'm going to lock up the IV pad so that you can't attempt to alter it and I'm going to ensure that a nurse watches you when we obtain any specimens because even though you may be sick this time, old habits die hard. You've been doctor-shopping this week, possibly with good reason, but the simple fact is that you cannot be relied on to tell the truth or to protect yourself from harm, so I'm going to do my best to minimise any temptations. Now, I'm being frank with you and I expect the same in return, OK?'

'OK.'

'Now, you're right, I don't expect the surgeons to come rushing to see you—they're up on the ward with a very sick patient at the moment and they've got another one that needs to go to Theatre soon—so I've decided to give you an anti-emetic and a small dose of morphine just to take the edge off. I won't give you much, so it will no doubt have worn off by the time you've had your CT and then the surgeons can see you and assess you properly.'

'Thank you.'

'Do you believe her,' Guy asked as Madison headed over to the drug cupboard, calling Alanna over as she did so to check the controlled drug with her.

'Yes,' Madison admitted. 'But I've believed her on many occasions and been proved wrong. If anything, she's not as convincing today as she has been in the past. She's given so many Oscar-winning performances...'

'Judith Baker!' Alanna said, rolling her eyes. 'The hospital is only two days old and already she's trying it on. Mind you, I'm surprised she wasn't waiting on the doorstep when we opened yesterday, hoping to convince someone she hadn't seen before that she was really sick this time.'

'It looks as if she could be genuinely ill this time,' Madison said, as Guy picked up the phone to ring the lab, but Alanna just groaned.

'Last year, at my old hospital, she was rushed to Theatre ahead of a five-year-old with appendicitis, and while she was being operated on, for what turned out to be nothing, the poor kid perforated. It was touch and go—all thanks to Judith.'

'I know,' Madison said wearily, pulling out the drugs and checking them with Alanna. 'But she is still a patient and sadly Judith is her own worst enemy. I've warned her over and over that one day she's desperately going to need help and no one's going to believe her. I've a feeling this time is it.'

As predicted by Guy, the surgeons didn't exactly drop everything when they were informed that Judith Baker was waiting to be seen. In an unfortunate turn of events, it was the very surgeon who had unwittingly put her ahead of the little boy with appendicitis the previous year who was the surgeon on take that morning. Checking Judith's obs, Madison didn't like the picture that was being painted, didn't like what she was seeing.

'Get Guy—now,' Madison called to Alanna, snapping off the gurney brakes with her foot and guiding the trolley out of cubicle two and over to Resus. Thankfully he was in the corridor and already coming over, and from the expression on his face he had clearly been anticipating the sudden commotion.

'Let's get her straight over,' he said, steering the trolley, deftly pulling an oxygen mask from the wall and placing it over Judith's mouth, even though she was still complaining loudly about the pain she was in.

'Her temperature and blood pressure have dropped,' Madison explained, turning on monitors and attaching red dots to her chest, then connecting the leads to them to give a cardiac tracing of her heart. She noted that Judith's heart rate was extremely rapid.

'I just came off the phone from the CT department. She's got a large collection in her abdomen, probably pus. She's going into septic shock. Alanna, page the surgeons and tell them to get down here now. And while you're on the phone, page the theatre sister and tell her to expect an urgent laparoscopy.' His orders were rapid, all delivered as he opened packs, giving out instructions to the gathering staff yet somehow finding the time to reassure Judith.

'Judith, I need to get some more fluid into you and I don't hold out much hope of finding another vein quickly so I'm going to put in a central line. Do you know what that is?'

'A line in my neck.' Judith's eyes were wide with fear, her grey face beading with sweat. Perhaps she realised that this time, it really was a genuine medical crisis she was experiencing.

Though Madison didn't understand her, even if Judith had brought this on herself, that wasn't the issue. Judith was her patient, desperately ill and terribly scared, and as the team swung into action, Madison took a moment to hold Judith's hand amidst the controlled chaos and offer some emotional support as Guy laid her flat and started to swab her neck with an iodine solution.

'You have a nasty pocket of infection in your stomach, so I'm going to get some fluids and antibiotics into you. The surgeons are going to take you to Theatre to drain the infection and find out where it's coming from.'

'I'm scared.' Judith's admission stilled his busy hand for a second, the years of bravado of playing Russian roulette with her life finally catching up with her.

'I know you are, Judith. But we're going to sort this out as best we can.'

'You believe me?' Judith begged, her greying face flailing on the pillow, a dry tongue licking even drier lips. 'I really didn't do it this time. I was working so hard on getting better.'

He nodded, his gloved hand cupping her cheek. 'You really don't want to be here, do you?'

'No!'

'Hey.' A smile dusted his lips. 'Today you might just find out how good we really are.'

'The nursing supervisor's on the phone for you, Madison.' Alanna dashed in and, seeing what Guy was doing, started to open a flask of IV solution to run through the central line. 'She wants to speak with you.'

'Tell her I'm busy,' Madison answered. 'I'll call her back when I can.'

'I've got this,' Alanna answered, and though she was trying to be helpful, and Madison knew that the situation was now completely under control, she wanted to stay. Wanted to be looking after her patient, not on the phone with the nursing supervisor, trying to juggle the bed status of the hospital and get patients up to the wards.

'Alanna?' Guy said, clearly clueless about the internal struggle taking place in Madison right now. 'Could you take off Judith's oxygen for a couple of moments? I want to get some blood gases from her on air.'

'I'll do it…' Madison started, reaching for the oxygen mask, but her hands met Alanna's at the same time. Jerking her eyes upwards, she saw Guy watching her.

A tiny frown crinkled the edges of his eyes, an instinctive understanding connecting them just for a moment.

She wanted to be nursing—not organising.

Trying to concentrate on paperwork was hell on earth. Despite her closed door, the department buzzed on outside Madison's office. The loudspeaker paging doctors, the swish of rubber heels running, babies crying, unattended IV machines bleeping. In an effort to help, Madison dragged her paperwork out to the nurses' station where she could at least take a few essential phone calls and direct the traffic somewhat, but before she knew it, she was giving out medication and handing out bedpans, ringing X-Ray to find out about delays and generally getting into the thick of things.

'You've got to deliver a welcome at orientation day.' Annie, the ward clerk, breezed in, peeling sheets of paper off a pile and trying to hand them to Madison.

'Orientation day?' Madison frowned, barely looking up as she took a student nurse through the rudimentaries of running through the IV that the doctor in cubicle four was shouting for.

'For the nursing bank,' Annie patiently explained. 'Shirley wants a senior staff member from each department to talk to the new bank staff to explain what each unit requires—what we want from the personnel in Emergency to make the department run more smoothly.'

'I'd settle for just an appearance right now,' Guy fumed, missing half of the conversation but making his feelings very much known as he punched in the switchboard number. 'I'm doing this well out of Judith's ear-shot—she's scared enough already, and if you don't like bad language, ladies, I suggest you leave now. I will not be hung up on or fobbed off again by some adolescent intern, telling me to check my patient's records.'

'You're going to be late,' Annie warned Madison, completely ignoring Guy, used to doctors blowing off a bit of steam. 'You're expected in five minutes.'

'Is it the orientation day?' Alanna asked as she breezed into the nurses' station, handing Guy a print-out of Judith's latest observations as he again attempted to contact the surgeons.

'It is,' Madison said grimly. 'To tell the truth, what with Gerard and trying to get the department up and running, I totally forgot about it. I haven't prepared a thing.'

'Just make sure you're not too nice!' Alanna said with a wry smile. 'I sometimes think we bend over so far backwards to make people think that Emergency's easy, in the hope of getting staff, that we omit to warn them how diverse and demanding the work can be. And in the end we both come out losers—we carry someone unsuitable for an entire shift and they in turn never want to set foot in the place again…' A blush darkened her cheeks and Alanna gave an apologetic wince. 'Sorry, I'll get off my soapbox now. It's nothing to do with me.'

'But it is,' Madison pointed out. 'You're a senior staff member, Alanna.' Taking a deep breath, she eyed her colleague. 'How would you feel about going to deliver the welcome? After all, you sound a lot more prepared than I am. Only if you don't mind, of course,' she added hastily, not wanting to pass the buck, but Alanna was good at this type of thing and if she wanted to do it, Madison was only too happy to delegate.

'I'd love to.' Alanna flushed. 'So long as you don't think…'

'I can't run this place on my own,' Madison said softly. 'And somehow go to every last meeting and deal single handed with every crisis that blows up. I need senior staff that I can rely on, senior staff who are willing to take the lead. And you're right up there, Alanna.'

'I don't give a damn,' Guy shouted down the telephone, after three prolonged calls. 'It doesn't matter what she's done in the past, the fact is this woman is ill, mentally and this time physically…' He paused and Madison found she was holding her breath, watching Guy's grim face on the phone as he insisted that the surgical registrar again drop what he was doing, again leave an unwell patient, to see a woman who had let them all down badly in the past.

'Let's cut the rubbish,' Guy broke in. 'You are a registrar, and, as of ten minutes ago, I am acting director of Emergency, and I am telling you to come down here urgently. In fact, I am going to hang up now and put out an emergency page for the surgeons to come to Emergency. And if you don't *run* to get here, you won't just have me to answer to.'

And he did just that. Terminated the call then

punched in triple zero, telling the switchboard operator to urgently summon the surgical team.

'Overkill?' He grimaced replacing the receiver.

'No.' Madison shook her head. 'The terrible thing is, I can see both sides. The surgeons have believed her over and over again, they've put her ahead of genuine patients and in some instances the consequences have been dire. But Trevor Jordan is a good man and he doesn't deserve to carry the guilt that's surely going to follow if he doesn't treat Judith promptly. And as you pointed out, Judith isn't just physically sick, but mentally, too. As hard as it is to give sometimes, she deserves our compassion and professionalism, whether or not she's faking it.'

'Did you rehearse that?' Guy blinked, a smile breaking out on his worried face.

'Sort of,' Madison admitted. 'I've been going over and over in my head how we should be dealing with Judith, and that's the best I could come up with.'

'Well, it helped,' Guy said, grimacing as the overhead chimes went off and the loudspeaker boomed out that surgeons were urgently required in Emergency. 'Thanks.'

'Acting director?' Madison asked as Guy swung down from his stool and headed into cubicle two.

'I just found out,' Guy said, his voice almost apologetic. 'I was going to tell you well away from here. You deserved to hear it properly, given you're the NUM. I just had to flex a few muscles to get Trevor down here.'

'That's fine,' Madison said, and as he headed off, she managed a tiny croak. 'Congratulations.'

'Madison?' A sharp rap on her office door was the only warning Madison had that Guy was coming in before the door opened. 'Are you busy?'

It was a pretty stupid question, given she was head down in a pile of paperwork and juggling a telephone call to the nursing administrator, trying to get an extra nurse for the late shift. But instead of giving a smart reply, Madison gestured for him to sit down and attempted to finish her call. Attempted, because the brisk, efficient person she'd been only a moment ago seemed to have lost track of the conversation. Even though Madison was more than familiar with having her conversations interrupted and doctors arriving unannounced and requiring her attention, in this instance even the most mundane of tasks—breathing—was proving difficult. Brutally aware of Guy's presence, she tried to refocus on the voice in her ear and block out the masculine scent filling her nostrils, the heavy scrutiny of his eyes on hers. When his pager shrilled, she had to physically drag her eyes away from the sight of his hand scribbling on a pad on her desk, suntanned hands with very short, very white, very neat nails.

'If I don't have an extra nurse, we'll have to go on bypass,' Madison insisted, referring to a situation where ambulances were rerouted to another hospital, a situation that was clearly far from ideal. 'I need a nurse by three p.m. at the latest,' Madison went on, rolling her eyes at Guy. 'Of course I'll let Dr Boyd know the situation. I'd appreciate it if you can get back to me as soon as possible.'

He gave a wry smile as she replaced the receiver.

'That was the nursing supervisor,' Madison explained, 'trying to give me a valid reason why we can't have one nurse to cover the three staff that I haven't got tonight. Given you're the consultant in charge today, she asked me to let you know what was going on.'

'Do you think we'll have to go on bypass?'

'No. They can "maybe" get a nurse to come at six p.m., but they're not prepared to pay overtime.'

'So how can we cover the department?' Guy frowned. 'The early staff finish at four…'

'I can stay back.' Madison shrugged.

'Shouldn't you be at home?' Guy frowned and so did Madison. The insinuation that she was putting the department before her daughter stung deeply, but just as quickly as it had started the tiny confrontation was over. Guy swiftly and appropriately moved the conversation from personal to professional. 'How come we're short?' As Madison opened her mouth to answer he put up his hand. 'That was probably the dumbest question I could have asked.'

'Probably,' Madison replied. 'Not all of the staff that have been recruited could start straight away, I've got one nurse who hurt her neck during the "back safe" demonstration, not to mention the staff we haven't yet been able to recruit. There's actually an advert coming out in a British newspaper this weekend, trying to wow nurses to come and nurse in sunny Australia.'

'Which smacks of robbing Peter to pay Paul. Sorry.' He gave a weak smile. 'I worked in the UK for a year and, believe me, their problems are much the same. Anyway…' his smile faded '…that isn't what I came in here to talk about.'

'About Judith?' Madison asked, but Guy shook his head.

'Nope, she's finally in Theatre.'

Taking a deep breath, Madison looked squarely back at him. 'You've heard from the pathologist about Gerard.'

Guy nodded.

'Have you spoken to Yvonne?'

'The pathologist rang her first with his findings. I'm not going to make this public, that has to be Yvonne's call, but given you were the one who was there when it happened and were involved in the attempted resuscitation, I figure that you deserve to know what happened as soon as possible.'

'Thank you.'

'Gerard suffered a massive cardiac event.' He closed his eyes for just a fraction too long, his voice slightly hoarse when he carried on. 'There was absolutely nothing that anyone could have done.'

'Nothing?' Madison checked, because it mattered, mattered more than she had let on yesterday, because Gerard had deserved the very best.

'Nothing,' Guy confirmed. 'I started to ask the pathologist that if we had somehow managed to revive him, what the outcome would have been—but he stopped me right there. He told me in no uncertain terms that Gerard had had a massive fatal heart attack, that there were no ifs or buts. He could not have survived under any circumstances. There was absolutely no chance of reviving him, none whatsoever. As you said yourself yesterday, Gerard was dead before he even hit the floor.'

'He didn't even complain of chest pain.' Madison's voice was dazed. 'If he had, if I'd thought for a moment—'

'Don't.' Guy shook his head. 'Don't go there, Madison.' His pager buzzed again and Guy grimaced as he read the message. 'Damn.'

'Problem?'

'Only that the CEO of the hospital shouldn't have to page me twice. Can I borrow your phone?' Picking it up without waiting for her answer, he punched in the numbers and listened more than spoke, finally putting down the receiver.

'The funeral is going to be on Thursday at ten a.m. Doug has said that any staff who want to go can attend and not to worry about the budget, to arrange cover…'

'That's a first.' Madison managed a wintry smile. 'We should be OK. Only a few of the staff worked with Gerard, most had only just met him. I'm sure everyone will be willing to shuffle the off-duty for one day, and I can always work the floor.'

'You?' Guy's voice was slightly incredulous. 'You're not going to go?'

'I'm needed here,' Madison said stiffly, but, realising something more was probably called for, she gave a tight shrug. 'I don't like funerals. I don't do very well at them.'

'Nobody likes funerals, Madison,' Guy responded sharply. 'But you're the nurse unit manager, for goodness' sake. Of course you have to go. You're expected—'

'Expected to what?' Jumping up, Madison clutched the desk, her knuckles as white as her pale lips, her fight-or-flight response so extreme Guy actually ducked back in his seat, his eyes wide as she continued. 'Expected to stand there and shed a dignified tear, to get up and give a speech about how he touched so many lives, expected to represent the hospital…'

'I know he was your friend.' Visibly shocked at her tirade, Guy's voice was kinder now, trying to calm her, trying to say the right thing. 'I know what happened yesterday was awful, I know that Gerard was more than a colleague to you, that he was a friend as well, but given that surely he'd want…' And on and on he went, trying and failing to say the right thing, missing the mark over and over until finally she halted him in utter defeat, sitting back down on her chair, appalled at having lost control like that, appalled at letting Guy, letting anyone, glimpse that painful, raw part of her soul, but knowing it deserved explanation.

'This isn't about Gerard.' She couldn't even look at him, so instead she closed her eyes to allow herself to continue. 'As selfish as it sounds, it's all about me.' She could feel the sweat beading on her forehead, feel her breath coming in short, unyielding gasps, and even though she'd never experienced a panic attack, this was as close as Madison wanted to come to having one. Almost choking to get the words out, infinitely grateful when Guy came over, sat on the desk right in front of her and took her trembling hand, she attempted to continue.

'The last funeral I went to was five years ago.'

'Go on,' Guy said, but it wasn't urgent. He handed her a glass of water from her desk and waited as she took a sip. 'Whose funeral was it?'

'My husband's,' Madison answered, her voice curiously detached now. 'He was killed in a motorbike accident.'

'I'm so sorry.'

'Emily was just a baby.' Urgent eyes turned to his. 'I haven't been to a funeral since. I'm terrified how I'm going to be. I feel awful because since yesterday, instead of mourning Gerard, I've been worrying about me…'

'Madison.' Guy's voice was firm. 'You don't have to go. I was talking through my hat before.'

'You're not wearing one.'

'No.' Guy smiled softly. 'Would you rather I said I was talking through my backside?'

'No.' Only then did she realize he was still holding her hand. His was dry and warm, hers cold and horribly, embarrassingly clammy, and she pulled it away. But even if they were talking about nothing, it helped more than she could believe, his vague, gentle teasing enough to bring her back to earth, a tiny interlude as everything settled, if not quite as it had been before, at least back into some sort of order.

'I've got to get back out there,' Guy said, gesturing to the door but clearly reluctant to leave without offering some sort of solution. 'Look, it's impossible to talk properly here. Why don't we go out for a drink tonight, grab some dinner?'

'There's nothing to talk about,' Madison answered coolly, but inside she was horribly flustered. The thought of facing him socially, away from the safety of the hospital, terrified her.

'I think there is,' Guy answered, looking directly at her. And something in his eyes, his voice, his stance told her he wasn't referring to Gerard, or funerals, or work, but to them—to the chemistry that had sparked between them, to the irrefutable tension that crackled whenever they were together. 'I'd like to get to know you, Madison, away from here. It's only dinner…'

But it wasn't only dinner, Madison knew that, knew that despite the casual offer, despite his attempt to soften the offer with an *only,* it had all the hallmarks of a date. A real-life grown-up date. Staring back at him, watching his soft blond hair falling over his forehead, those gorgeous hazel eyes taking in every flicker of her reaction, the delicious male scent of him filling the room, for a frighteningly long moment she was tempted to accept, to throw caution to the winds and just move with her feelings. But as the reason she would *have* to decline popped into her mind, it was as if a bucket of icy water had been poured over her—feelings, emotion that had struggled towards the surface firmly quashed as common sense took over, as the practicalities of being a mother, a widow, a working woman mocked her temporary moment of recklessness.

'In case it slipped your mind, I've got a daughter, Guy. I think I used up all my babysitting tokens long ago.'

'Tokens?'

'Favours,' Madison briskly corrected. 'I can't just pull a childminder out of thin air.' Satisfied she'd given a dignified no, Madison picked up her pen, effectively ending the conversation, but still Guy remained.

'Bring her along,' Guy offered.

Madison's pen froze mid-signature, internally damning him through gritted teeth, but forcing a smile instead.

'I don't think so.'

'You don't think so?' Guy smiled, ever the optimist. 'Is that a maybe?'

'It's a no,' Madison said firmly.

'So you're just going to sit home alone tonight and mull things over, work yourself into a tizz about the funeral—'

'Again,' Madison broke in, 'you exemplify how little you know about my life, Guy. After I've collected Emily, made her dinner, helped her with her homework, bathed her, set out both our uniforms for tomorrow, listened to her read, then read to her, maybe, just maybe, I'll have half an hour to myself before collapsing into bed, only to get up a few hours later and do it all over again!'

She was painting a picture, trying to show him the impossibility of her situation, to scare him off perhaps, but infuriatingly he still stood there, still smiled that lazy smile at her.

'Anyway,' Madison carried on, 'I've made up my mind and I'm going to go.'

'To dinner?'

'To the funeral,' Madison said, despite her words, somehow smiling.

'You don't have to.'

'I actually want to,' Madison admitted. 'I want to say goodbye to Gerard and I want to lay a few ghosts of my own to rest. I'm just worried I'll make a fool of myself.'

'I'll stay with you,' Guy said firmly, and Madison frowned at the possibility, frowned at the prospect of actually leaning on someone. 'I'll stay with you the whole time. You don't have to do this on your own.'

'I'll be fine on my own.'

'You probably would,' Guy responded. 'Only you're not going to get a chance. I'll make sure that you don't have to do a reading or anything like that—all you have to do is be there. I'll pick you up at nine-thirty on Thursday.'

'You don't even know where I live.'

He stood up, shot her just a tiny glimpse of that devastating smile. 'Ah, but as acting director, I'm sure I'll be able to find out.'

CHAPTER FOUR

'IF THERE'S a heaven, why do people cry when some-one dies?'

'Because they miss them,' Madison answered, her throat thickening, wishing Emily would just buckle up her seat belt so she could get her to school.

Wishing that this whole day was over with.

'Do you miss Daddy?'

Aware of two very beady eyes staring at her in the rear-view mirror, Madison resisted the urge to grimace. Instead, she took a deep breath and then gave a long, slow nod. 'Of course I do. And,' she added, because this conversation wasn't really about her, but about her daughter, 'I'm sure that Daddy misses you, too.'

'But can he see me?'

'He can.' Madison gulped.

'He knows I'm OK?'

'He does,' Madison said, wishing fiercely that Emily would change the subject. 'And I'm sure he's really proud of you.'

'You should get a new boyfriend— Mummy, you've stalled the car!'

Be careful what you wish for, Madison thought, slamming her foot on the clutch and restarting the engine.

'Helen's got a new boyfriend.'

'Has she?' Madison asked, frantically revving the car. 'Who told you?'

'Richard—but he's not allowed to know yet, so you mustn't say a word. All the grey hairs on Helen's head have gone blonde and Richard heard her talking on the telephone, saying that she's going out on Friday and that she hopes it's somewhere expensive! He's got the same job as Jesus.'

'Who has?' Madison asked faintly, doing bunny-hops all the way to school.

'Helen's new boyfriend. He's a carpenter!'

'OK?'

Opening her door, she was greeted by the single word, and even though Madison automatically nodded, midway it changed and she gave a tight shrug. 'I don't actually know.'

'You'll be fine,' Guy said softly. 'And if you're not, I've got a very good plan B.'

'Plan B?' Madison frowned.

'If it looks like you're about to lose it, I'll save you the embarrassment and pretend to faint or something— everyone will be so busy looking at me, they'll forget about you.'

'Please,' Madison scoffed, but amazingly her pale face, for the first time that hateful morning, was smiling. 'Come in. I'm nearly ready.'

Holding the door open, she stood back as he walked in, her generous hallway seeming to shrink as Guy walked down it. Until now she'd only ever seen him in either jeans or theatre greens, but dressed in a black suit, his unruly blond hair neatly combed, still damp from the shower, and even in Madison's tense, introspective state, there was no denying Guy looked stunning. His broad shoulders seemed to fill the hallway, his features were accentuated more with his hair slicked back, and when he entered her living room, and turned and smiled at her, Madison could feel her breath catching in her throat.

'You have a nice home.'

'Thank you,' Madison responded to the pleasantry, but Guy was still looking around, taking in the scattered bright cushions on the sofa, the jumble of crayons and picture books on the coffee-table, framed photographs adorning every available surface.

'I mean that, it's a real home.'

'Of course it is.' Madison gave a slightly nervous laugh. 'What were you expecting?'

'I don't know,' Guy admitted. 'Something more…' he gave a helpless shrug '…immaculate, I guess. Not that it's untidy or anything,' he added quickly. 'I guess, from the way your office is, the way you are at work, I figured your home would be the same.'

'This *is* immaculate.' Madison smiled. 'For me, anyway. I tidied up for two hours last night because you were coming. I'm a control freak at work, not at home. Believe me, when you're sharing a house with a five-year-old, you soon learn to let go.' She gave a dry smile, remembering that morning's conversation with her daughter, and suddenly, inexplicably almost, wanted to share it with Guy, but sensibly chose not to. 'Do you want a coffee?' Madison asked. 'We've got plenty of time.'

'Do you?'

'Yes,' Madison admitted. 'I'd rather be nervous here than there.' He followed her into the kitchen, leaning against the bench and watching as she spooned coffee and sugar into cups, noting at first her jerky, nervous movements, but more, more than that, he noticed the bright paintings on the fridge, no doubt done by her daughter. The whiteboard above the telephone accounted for every moment of every day, and as she opened the cupboard to pull out sugar to top up the sugar bowl, he couldn't help but see that, aside from the crisps and biscuits, the children's cereal and all the paraphernalia that lived in a working mother's kitchen cupboards, on one lonely shelf stood an endless row of meals for one, the same meals he's watched her throw in the microwave at lunchtime. Something told him the same thing happened in the evenings.

'How are you doing with this?' Madison asked, when finally they were seated in the lounge, her eyes nervously darting towards the clock, knowing that in a short space of time they would have to leave, have to face what she was dreading. 'From the way Gerard spoke of you, you were pretty close. Did you work together?'

'Once formally,' Guy replied. 'But over the last few years I've called on him hundreds of times, either by phone or the internet, for advice. I've done a lot of AID work overseas. I'm sure that you don't need me to tell you how generous Gerard was with his knowledge— I could always call on him. It's a shame we didn't get to work together again. I was really looking forward to it.'

'Was that why you took the job—to work alongside Gerard?' Madison asked. 'I mean, if you've worked overseas, seen so much, a suburban hospital is hardly going to be cutting edge.'

'That was part of the reason, and a new hospital opens up an interesting set of challenges, which are appealing. I guess I figured that it will look good on my résumé,' Guy admitted. 'Though I have to say, after years of tarpaulin and mosquito nets, the thought of a key to my own front door, constant running hot water— even a mortgage—has actually started to appeal.'

'You've had enough of travelling?' Madison asked.

'For now.'

'So, how come you settled here? Are your family in Melbourne?'

'No.' Fiddling with his coffee-cup, Guy shook his head, and even though he clearly didn't want to talk about his reasons for settling, Madison was scared he'd look at his watch and decide that it was time to go. Taking a deep breath, despite Guy's reluctance to prolong the conversation, Madison pushed on anyway.

'So where are they?' Madison asked. As his shoulders stiffened, she immediately regretted her insensitivity. 'Your family?'

'There's only my mother,' Guy responded stiffly. 'She's in India—again.'

'Oh.'

'Apparently she's "finding herself".'

'Oh.' Madison blinked, not really knowing what to say, but Guy now had plenty.

'One would have hoped that by the time you reached fifty-two, you'd have "found yourself", wouldn't you?' His eyes jerked to hers and Madison found herself frowning at the pain behind his voice.

'You'd hope so,' she said tentatively. 'What does your mother do—for a living, I mean?'

'She's a doctor. She specialises in tropical and infectious diseases.'

'Is that how you got into AID work?'

'I've been into it since I was six months old,' Guy responded. When Madison's eyebrows shot up somewhere into her hairline, he elaborated further. 'Mum was into AID work before it was even remotely trendy. She's done a lot in Papua New Guinea and some of the small islands. Most of the time she took me with her.'

'But what about school?'

'There were teachers here and there, a lot of books. Mum's extremely clever—she taught me well, though, thankfully when I was sixteen I boarded here in Melbourne, which meant I could concentrate on getting good enough grades to study medicine.'

Which was no mean feat. Places at medical school were exceptionally hard to come by, and to get in with only two years of formal education was nothing short of amazing.

'So you don't actually have relatives here in Melbourne?' Madison asked, and for some reason she didn't want to fathom, the question unnerved her. If he had no one here, there really wasn't much reason to stay, and there was something about Guy, something about this confident yet closed man that intrigued her, something about him that evoked a response she hadn't felt in a long, long time.

He paused for a long time before answering, enough time for Madison to process her jumbled thoughts, to realise that she actually wanted him to stay, wanted to get to know him better. 'There's no one,' he said finally. Looking at his watch, she could almost feel the sigh of relief from him that this conversation was over, that now he could legitimately stand up and tell her that they had better get going.

Pulling on some black court shoes, Madison checked her lipstick in the hall mirror, rued the fact she had even bothered with mascara and fiddled with her hair for a moment. Guy stood patiently at the door, perhaps sensing that it had nothing to do with vanity and everything to do with remaining in control, with taking care of the small details and hoping that if she did, the bigger ones would fall into place.

'Ready?'

Tears flashed in her eyes as she nodded and headed for the front door, her hands shaking so much she could barely lock the blessed thing behind her. She joined him in his dark sports car and felt the tension increasing as he switched on the engine and they drove the short distance to the church. The street was packed with cars, endless people were milling around in dark suits, even darker glasses shielding both tears and the harsh Australian morning sun. Madison rummaged in her handbag for her own sunglasses, noting that Guy already had his on. Staring down at his hands, she saw the white of his knuckles as he gripped the steering-wheel and it wasn't just about herself any more and how she was going to get through this, but about Guy, too, about a man who had also lost a friend and colleague.

'Let's do this,' she whispered, opening the car door and stepping out, waving and talking in a subdued voice to the endless stream of familiar faces. All of them wanted to be here, but not one of whom could quite believe that they really were.

And, as most fears were, when faced head on, it wasn't bad. It was awful and sad, but it wasn't the nightmare Madison had envisaged. Surprising herself, she managed to sing along to the hymns, focussing on Gerard instead of her own painful memories. Exquisitely aware of Guy standing straight and tall next to her, they read from the same hymn book, Guy holding it, Guy turning the page, so all Madison had to do was concentrate on herself, drawing strength from his presence, glad that someone knew her plight. She was able to finally relax enough to listen as Gerard's son rose to speak about his father, even managing a smile as somehow he managed to capture some of Gerard's funnier traits. She looked at Guy and was appalled to see a tear rolling down his cheek, could feel the tension in his body. In an instinctive gesture her hand reached out to his, her fingers coiling around his. She bit her lip as for a fleeting second he held on.

'I'll be fine.' Guy gave a stiff nod as he mouthed the words, reclaiming his hand and staring fixedly ahead. 'I'll be fine.'

'Here.' Pressing a massive brandy into Madison's hand, Guy nodded a greeting to a couple of people he must have recognised, before turning his attention back to Madison. A buffet and drinks had been put on at the hospital, but now an invited few were back at the family home and Madison watched as Guy fiddled with his black tie, clearly uncomfortable, the small talk having dried up long ago. 'How long do you think we should stay?'

'Not long,' Madison answered, looking around at the thinning crowd. 'In fact, I think it might be appropriate if we leave now.'

'You don't mind?' Guy checked. 'I only just got you a drink.'

'I've had two brandies already on the emptiest stomach in the world. I'm certainly not going to get through this one!'

'Right, let's say goodbye, then.'

The farewells were difficult somehow. Even though Madison knew she had done everything she could to help Gerard, Yvonne's obvious discomfort as she and Guy approached caused a pang of anxiety as Madison said goodbye.

'You did your best,' Yvonne said kindly. 'You did everything humanly possible, and for that we're very grateful.'

'Thank you.' Madison dusted Yvonne's cheek with her lips. 'I'm so sorry for your loss.'

She waited for Guy, stood at the door expecting to stand for a couple of moments as he said his goodbyes, but after a brief handshake with Gerard's son and a small murmur of farewell to Yvonne, Guy was beside her, taking her arm and leading her out to the car.

'Is everything—?'

'Everything's fine,' Guy answered stiffly, but Madison wasn't convinced, and once they were seated in the car, before he turned on the engine Madison voiced what was on her mind.

'Is she upset with us, Guy? Do you think she somehow blames us for not doing more?'

'I don't know.' Guy shrugged. 'Look, Yvonne and I...' His jaw clenched, his mouth snapping closed on the words. 'She doesn't blame you at all, Madison, no one does.'

'But she was so wooden, so—'

'She just lost her husband,' Guy snapped, then instantly regretted it. 'Look, Madison, it's me she doesn't like, not you.'

And though she'd have loved to have asked more, something in Guy's expression told her the subject was closed, something in his stance told her to leave things well alone.

They drove in tense silence to Madison's house and, despite the relief that the hard part of the day was over, all of a sudden Madison didn't want it to end. Turning shyly to him, she offered him coffee.

'I'm not much company at the moment,' Guy responded.

'Neither am I.' Madison smiled. 'We can be morose together.'

The awful thing about funerals, Madison decided, was that they were generally held in the morning. In some ways it served its purpose, meant that you didn't spend the whole day dreading the event, but because it was a funeral, because it was such a big event, the whole day was generally set aside to accommodate it. Helen was giving Emily dinner tonight so she had the whole afternoon and evening to fill, and as Madison stepped back into her home with Guy it seemed almost incomprehensible that it was only just two o'clock. The house was impossibly warm and Madison flicked on the air-conditioner, the whirring sound breaking the oppressive silence. 'I'll make us some coffee,' Madison said as Guy sat down on the sofa, loosening his tie as if it were choking him.

'What time do you pick your daughter up from school?'

'I'm not—my friend is having her for dinner.'

He didn't say anything, but she could almost feel the tiny sting of condemnation that beat in the air, and even though Madison didn't have to justify herself to anyone, least of all Guy Boyd, she wanted to.

'I don't usually rely so heavily on my friend, Guy. This week was always going to be difficult, and I'd made arrangements in advance for Emily to spend some extra time at Helen's.'

'I didn't say anything,' Guy pointed out, but Madison stopped him right there.

'You didn't have to. Guy, I'm a single mother and I owe it to my daughter to give her a decent standard of living. I have to work, but I make sure I'm home a lot, too.'

'I know.' Guy nodded. 'I mean, I don't know, but I can see from this house, from the way you talk about her…' He gave a tight shrug. 'It's not for me to judge.'

'No, Guy,' Madison said firmly. 'It isn't.'

Going out to the kitchen, Madison set about making coffee, trying and failing not to let Guy's carefully unvoiced insinuation rile her.

Emily came first, last and always.

Emily was the reason she was stuck in an office half the day instead of being out on the floor. Emily was the reason she had striven for an NUM position, to enable her to be home in the mornings and evenings, to give her each and every weekend off. Madison forcibly pushed it all to one side, consoling herself that the most responsible thing Guy Boyd would ever have had to do was to remember to take his antimalaria tablets. What would a man like him know about mortgages and gas bills and dancing lessons? What would he know about rates and schoolbooks and the million and one things that were processed in a woman's life?

Hell, it was hot!

Peeling off her jacket, Madison looked down at the black camisole she was wearing, wondering if it was appropriate, then gave a tiny impatient shake of her head at her train of thought. Her trusty but rather old air-conditioner wasn't going to cool the place down in the next few minutes, and a lined suit was hard work at the best of times, let alone on a thirty-plus degree day. Slipping out of her shoes, Madison finally felt herself relax. Padding back to the living room in her stockinged feet, carefully balancing a tray, she saw Guy on the sofa and, despite the fact it was her own home, Madison felt as if she were somehow intruding, as if she were snooping, because, clearly not having heard her approach, Guy was sitting on the edge of the couch, his head in his hands, his shoulders slumped, such a picture of desolation her first instinct was to cross the room and comfort him. But instead she stepped back out of the doorway and gave a small cough to announce her arrival, and this time when she entered he was sitting up straight, a false, strained smile on his lips.

Kneeling down by the coffee-table, she attempted to spoon sugar into the coffee, but her hand was shaking so much she spilled most of it. She had a burning awareness of him behind her, and for the second time in as many minutes questioned her decision to wear only a camisole, because the burning weight of his eyes was scorching through the flimsy fabric on the back of her neck. And though she couldn't see him, as if by telepathy she could feel him, feel the presence of him, an awareness that engulfed her, the air so thick now she had to drag it into her lungs. She anticipated, before his fingers brushed the back of her neck, what was about to happen. As he traced the length of her neck, dusted his fingers over her shoulder, her first sensible thought was to jerk away, to demand that he stop, but a deeper instinct held her still, held her transfixed, almost willing his hand on, scared almost to move, to speak, to even breathe, scared to break the moment.

A delicious heat spread over her shoulders as his index finger traced her clavicle. It was the smallest, gentlest of touches, but it was exquisitely erotic, just the contact of his skin on hers, the tip of his finger over the flickering pulse in the hollow of her throat physically weakened her. Madison's eyes closed in silent acknowledgement of a basic, primitive need she had held back for so long now, one she had denied even existed. But as her face turned to him, as his strong silent eyes held her tremulous ones, the tension that had held her together to this point seemed to dissolve. Emotion she had pushed back for so long bubbled to the fore. Transfixed, she stared, a heady mixture of terror and excitement going through her as his lips moved toward hers. She could smell, taste the arousal in the air. Anticipating the weight of his mouth on hers, she parted her own lips slightly and took a tiny breath as the bruising feel of his mouth met hers, the scratch of his chin dragging her cheek, the sharp, unfamiliar taste of him, the cool of his tongue as gently he parted her lips further. And it didn't make sense, it could never be understood or explained to the rational side of her brain, but it felt so right.

So right to be held, to be kissed, to move her mouth with his, yielding to him, the delicious feel of his hands on her back, the tangy scent of him close up. It had been so long since she'd felt like this, so long since she'd been held with such passion and longing, and if they regretted it tomorrow, regretted it this day even, right now she didn't care. Right now all Madison wanted was to give in to her body, to dissolve in his arms, to be led by this delicious man, to let go of the pain that surrounded them for even just a little while.

'Madison?' His question was a throaty gasp. 'I want you…'

'I want you, too,' she whispered, taking control now.

She pulled at his tie, kissing him hungrily, the tiny buttons of his shirt somehow managed easily, exposing a delicious toned torso. He had a smattering of blond hair across his chest and circling the dark mahogany of his nipples. Slowly he slid the zipper of her camisole, his warm hand taking the weight of her breasts as the other undid the metal clasp of her bra. He made her feel beautiful. With every touch, every moan, every stroke of her flesh he dragged her reserve away, peeled away the inhibitions as easily as he peeled away their clothes. His trousers were tossed in a rumpled heap of hastily discarded clothing and need fuelled them, a need to see each other, to touch, to explore. Naked, he was so beautiful she almost wept at the feel of male flesh beneath her fingers, the quiet strength of being held, caressed, kissed, the salty taste of his skin, the thickening hair that directed her to his most intimate place.

Kneeling, she lifted her bottom as he slid her skirt down over her hips, his hand stroking the curve of her buttocks, twisting the knife of desire so taut she let out a low needy moan as his fingers slipped into her warmth, the pad of his finger pushing her in tiny deliberate strokes that had her head arching back, delicious tension tightening every muscle, filled with a need she hadn't known existed, had denied even to herself. Yet with one stroke of his hand, one taste of his cool, experienced mouth, he kindled a wantonness that had been kept in check for so long now, and revealed in a heartbeat the woman beneath the façade.

She revelled in it, so much that it was Madison who took things further, taking his manhood in her hands, feeling the heady weight of his erection nudging the sensitive skin of her inner thighs, and all she knew was that she needed more. Guy sensed it, holding her buttocks, guiding her down on his delicious length, moving her slowly, guiding her as she held on to his shoulders, the sheen of skin beneath her, the full swell of him within her. And it was like nothing she had ever felt before, an exquisite closeness she could never have imagined. Their bodies were in gentle tune, a deep knowing cloaking them, moving them to deeper union, guiding them to the very peak of pleasure. And he wasn't guiding her any more, his hands lost in her hair as they moved in sync, faster, deeper thrusts that made her cry out as a deep knotting tension grew inside her, her thighs tightening. Her hands moved to his shoulders as this elusive pleasure rippled through her body, gathering force as it went, a flood of heat dashing along her spine, stinging its way to the back of her neck, her whole body shuddering with the sheer delicious force of her orgasm.

It should have been over, she needed to catch her breath, to collapse on him in blessed relief. She'd given all of herself to him, but she wrestled to somehow still stay in control, fought for her head, but it was Guy pulling tightly on the reins, Guy taking the lead now. She could feel him tensing deep within her, feel deep, hard thrusts that filled her further, and instead of regaining control she lost it, years of holding it together deliciously abating as her pleasure grew, painful almost in its intensity, sheer abandonment in every pore as she gave in to him again, letting him take her higher, further, deeper than she had ever had been until her short neat nails dug into his wide shoulders as she cried out his name, gave that last piece of herself no one had ever witnessed until, gasping, exhausted, but sated with pleasure, she finally relaxed against him, heard the thudding of his heart as it beat loudly in her ear, the feel of his skin on her cheek as the world slowly stopped spinning.

'Guy?' Madison's bewildered voice was barely a

whisper, but he heard the question behind it, heard the doubt, the embarrassment, the regret in the single word.

'It's OK,' he said quickly, but she shook her head, unable to look at him, completely unable to lift her head, to stare into his eyes and acknowledge what had taken place. But he pulled her back, lifted her chin to force her to look at him. 'It's OK, Madison, there's nothing to regret.'

'Oh, but there is…' Pulling herself up, she rummaged for her clothes, pulling on her knickers, trying to force her damp, flushed body into her camisole, to pull up her zipper, and somehow avoid his eyes. 'Guy, I've got a five-year-old daughter. What just happened was beyond irresponsible, it was completely out of character—'

'It was inevitable,' Guy broke in, pulling on his boxer shorts before standing up to face her. 'Madison, you can't deny that there's a huge attraction between us.'

'There isn't.' Vehemently she shook her head, furiously she denied it. 'I'm not attracted to—' Madison started, realising the sheer futility of her words. The evidence was irrefutable and as her voice trailed off Guy gave a slow lazy smile.

'So you usually make wild, uninhibited love with men you're not in the least bit attracted to, do you?' A very reluctant smile wobbled on her lips, her eyes closing in embarrassment as Guy carried on talking. 'Madison, I'm not even going to try denying that I'm attracted to you, I'm not going to pretend for a moment that I didn't want to sleep with you, but what I will tell you is that not for a moment did I expect it to happen today. I didn't come here with the intention of sleeping with you. I came here because I wanted to be with you, wanted to get to know you a bit better.'

'Then how?' Genuinely bewildered, she blinked back at him, scarcely able to comprehend what had just taken place, how in the space of an afternoon her safe ordered word had disappeared, that she had slept with not just a man she barely knew but a man she would be working with. A man whose respect she should command, a man who, day in day out, she would have to face.

'It just happened, Madison.' Guy answered as if that were explanation enough but, seeing the confusion in her eyes, he crossed the room, took her stunned face in his hands and continued, 'Madison, sometimes these things just happen…'

'Not to me!' Appalled, she wrenched herself away. 'Not to me they don't, Guy. Look, I know you think I'm overreacting, I know I was a completely willing participant, it's just that…' Her mouth snapped closed, trapping feelings she didn't want to reveal, trying to save herself from exposing more than she already had.

But Guy refused to accept her silence, refused to accept her rejection. He put his hands on her shoulders and guided her to the sofa.

'Am I the first person you've slept with since your husband?' His hand tightened on her shoulders as she nodded reluctantly. He watched as a tear tumbled down her cheek despite her best efforts to squeeze it back, his thumb collecting a damp, loose strand of hair plastered to her forehead and smoothing it gently behind her ear. And if he hadn't been in his boxers he'd have tried to locate a handkerchief, but instead he watched as Madison gave a rather inelegant sniff and attempted to compose herself. Gently he ploughed on, trying to say the right thing. 'I wish I'd known that, known how hard this was for you—the guilt you must be feeling. All I can say is that I know this happened quickly, but it doesn't have to cheapen things. We just did it the wrong way around. Madison, I want to get to know you, all of you, I want to get close to you…' She frowned up at him, as if he were speaking a foreign language that she'd barely even started to grasp. But occasional words filtered through and, despite her utter confusion, somehow she understood what it was Guy was saying—because she wanted to get close to him, too, wanted to get to know him, all of him. Staring back at his gorgeous face, for a slice of time it almost seemed possible that with a man like Guy maybe they could work it out, maybe they could learn this language together. Perhaps sensing the shift in her, he pushed just a touch harder.

'Tonight.' He stroked her hair slowly. 'Tonight we'll…'

And like a balloon popping the hope, the possibility that had hung in the air dispersed and with a frustrated sob Madison wrenched herself away.

'How, Guy? Are you intending to take me out for dinner, to the movies perhaps, or maybe we can go clubbing? Did I omit to mention that I'm way out of babysitter tokens for the next six months?' He opened his mouth to object, but Madison was going full steam ahead, reaching for her shoes and pulling them on, as bitter, angry words spilled out of her mouth. 'Or perhaps I should go and pick up Emily and tell her that mummy has got a new boyfriend, why doesn't she come home and meet him?'

'Madison! You're being—'

'Ridiculous?' She nodded her head. 'Because it's ridiculous to even think for a moment that this could work. And you're wrong, Guy, it's not because of some rose-coloured view of my late husband that I haven't slept with anyone since he died, it's not because of some misguided sense of honour that I haven't hit the singles bars or nightclubs. It's because of the mess my husband left me to pick up when he died. The mess I've spent the last five years extricating myself from. Yes, I'm attracted to you, yes, given the emotion of today, perhaps the outcome was inevitable, but if you think I want flowers and meals to somehow dignify it, you're wrong. All I want is to put this behind us.'

'To pretend it didn't happen?' His voice was incredulous, scarcely able to comprehend the change that had taken place, that the warm, loving, sensual woman he had held only moments before could just get up and walk off, but Madison wasn't going to give in.

'We slept together, Guy. We're two consenting adults who slept together. It's no big deal.'

'You're a useless liar, Madison. That wasn't just sex for the sake of it, and you know it as well as I do! Where are you going?' he asked, following her out to the kitchen as she marched out and pulled on her shoes, headed to the hall mirror and dragged a comb through her dishevelled hair.

'I'm going to pick up my daughter, Guy.'

'Surely you've got five minutes?'

Madison glanced at her watch, appalled to see that she was already five minutes late—confirmation if ever she'd needed it that what she had contemplated for that brief moment was impossible. Emily deserved better. 'Actually, I don't.' Frantically she rubbed in foundation and tried to calm her flushed cheeks.

'Tomorrow, then?' Guy asked. 'When it's your lunch-break, we'll meet and talk.'

'I've got an appointment with my life coach tomorrow lunchtime.'

'Life coach?'

'Yes.' His bemusement irritated her. 'My life coach,' she repeated, as if it was self-explanatory.

'What is that? Come on, Madison, I've spent the last few years wandering the globe—what the hell's a life coach?'

'Someone who helps you to outline and achieve your goals.' He was standing behind her, frowning at her in the mirror, and Madison sucked in her breath, dragging out the words as if she were reading them from the glossy brochure that had dropped on her mat more than a year ago. 'Most people don't achieve their full poten-tial, most people wander through life with no plan. Kerry and I meet monthly and we work out my priorities, set goals, formulate a plan so that I can optimise my emotional and physical wellbeing.'

'You pay someone to work out your dreams?'

'No, Guy, I pay someone to help me achieve my goals.'

'Which are?'

'It's in the singular, Guy. I only have one goal and that's stability.' Madison stared back at him. 'Stability for my daughter.'

'And where do you come into this?' His lips were almost a sneer. 'When your life coach is busy working out your financial, physical and emotional wellbeing, where does Madison Walsh come into the picture? Where does the woman I held back there come into it?'

He had a point, but Madison had an answer.

'That comes under emotional wellbeing and, yes, we've addressed it, but I decided to put that on hold until I'd sorted out more pressing matters.'

A mirthless smile ghosted his lips. 'So a quick one will have to suffice for now?' His crudeness had Madison biting on her lip but she refused to let him see how much his words hurt. Instead she turned around and finally managed to face him.

'I guess it will. Now, if you'll excuse me, I have to collect my daughter.'

'Of course. I'll be out of here in a moment.' As she wrenched open the front door to flee down the drive, Guy caught her shoulder. 'Just think about us tonight.'

'Us?' She almost choked the word out—couldn't even turn around to look at him, every muscle rigid with tension.

'Us,' Guy repeated, as if 'us' already existed. 'Just think about what you're walking away from.'

Dashing over to Helen's, her trembling hand knocked on her friend's front door. Racked with guilt, she waited for the accusing stares, the suspicious looks, as if everyone must somehow know what had just taken place. But it was Madison's eyes that widened as Helen flung open the front door, wearing a dressing-gown that had seen better days and a vivid green face pack.

'It's supposed to shrink my pores,' Helen offered by way of explanation, padding down the hallway. 'The kids are just finishing up their homework so let's grab a quick cuppa while we've got time.'

'I'm sorry I'm late…' Madison said, blinking at the normality of it all, hearing the kids chatting in the lounge room, the evening news droning on, everything as it should be.

'Are you?' Helen gave a vague shrug. 'Don't give it a thought. How was it?' When Madison didn't answer, Helen pulled out some mugs and switched on the kettle, her face pack cracking as she gave Madison a sympathetic smile. 'It must have been hard—saying goodbye to someone you care about.'

'It was,' Madison said quietly, immersed in double meanings, her mind spinning from the emotionally draining day. 'It really was.'

CHAPTER FIVE

'YOU'VE had an exceedingly challenging week.' Kerry, Madison's life coach, leant back in her very nice navy leather chair and crossed her very neat legs. 'But you've coped admirably.' Shuffling through Madison's papers, she ticked off some boxes. 'Madison, you've done amazingly well. Your salary has increased enough to send your daughter to your chosen school, you've your own parking space, and you're even managing to go to the hospital gym for a workout twice a week, as well as walking with Emily some evenings. You've attained everything you set out to.'

'I guess.' Madison stared out of the massive window into the busy street below, watching an ambulance weaving through the early afternoon traffic, the thick, double-glazed window muting the wail of the siren. But Emily could see the flashing lights, the urgency of the vehicle as it picked its way around the slowing cars, and Madison wondered what was coming into the department, wanted to be down there, finding out. Instead, she darted her eyes away and looked over at

Kerry. 'The thing is—I don't actually need a parking space,' Madison gulped, watching as Kerry gave her a slightly perplexed look. 'I mean, it's nice and everything but, given the fact I'm not arriving with all the other early staff, I could quite easily find a spot to park. I don't really need my own parking space.'

'But it shows how well you're doing,' Kelly pointed out. 'The same way you can now comfortably afford to move Emily to the school you've chosen for her.'

'Even though Emily's happy at the school she's at?' Madison was as confused as Kerry. 'Maybe taking her out isn't such a good idea after all. I don't know why it seemed so important.'

'It was one of your goals,' Kerry pointed out, tapping the paperwork in front of her then handing it over to Madison.

Madison stared at her own handwriting, which said exactly the same thing, trying to remember a time when two yellow lines to park her car between had seemed so important, when a posh school with a boater for Emily to attend had seemed so vital, scarcely able to believe that the date above was only a month ago. 'And you've attained them. You should be feeling pretty pleased with yourself.'

'And I am.' Madison nodded, more to convince Kerry than herself, watching as she shuffled the paperwork in front of her and silently dreading what she knew was about to come.

'Now, we've addressed the financial and physical side of your life. You're in great shape in both areas, but it's time we looked at the emotional side of things. What are your goals there, Madison? Where do you see yourself in twelve months' time?'

'Coming off my shift to a graffitied car in my personal parking space and signing cheques to a school I can't actually afford, which my daughter doesn't want to go to…' As Kerry crossed and re-crossed her legs, stumbled for an answer to her client's inappropriate response, Madison gave a rather helpless laugh.

'I think the goalposts just moved.'

'That's why we meet regularly,' Kerry responded quickly. 'Life is an evolving process. Now that your financial and health needs are being met, now that there's order in your life, we can deal with the emotional aspects, find out what it is that Madison Walsh wants.'

'You mean, write out another list.' Madison frowned. 'List my ideal partner?'

'Not necessarily,' Kerry said. 'I'm not for a moment suggesting you can only be emotionally complete with a partner by your side. But your emotional needs do need to be addressed. Yes, you're a mother, yes, you have a demanding career, but you still need to nurture yourself. We can start off slowly, perhaps just meeting friends for coffee at the shopping centre, inviting some people over for a dinner party…'

But Madison wasn't even listening any more. As much of a help as Kerry had been, as much as she herself had needed the support to get her life in order, setting goals with her friends just sounded too clinical for words. Relegating her emotional wellbeing to a neat list of objectives took all the fun out of it somehow. She picked up her bag and stood up.

'Kerry, you've been great. My life was an absolute mess when I first came here, and you've helped me a lot. I've lost weight, toned up, I'm drinking soy milk and I'm finally in the black, but as for the emotional side…' Madison picked up the clipboard and stared at the unfilled boxes, the goals she should set out to attain, the ticks that would somehow decipher the perfect man in a perfect world, and knew that nothing she wrote there could even begin to explain her needs. 'I guess I'm going to have to leave that to a greater power…'

'One that doesn't charge eighty dollars an hour.' Kerry gave a thin smile, but it reached her eyes and for the first time in all the while she'd been there, Madison actually warmed to the other woman.

'I've met someone,' Madison admitted. 'Every pore in me is screaming that he's a wanderer, that say the C word and he'll walk. He's certainly not what I've got planned for Emily and I, and yet…' Her voice faltered for a moment but then she found it again. 'Yesterday I thought it was impossible, I told him it wasn't going to happen.'

'So what's changed?'

'He asked me to think about it,' Madison answered. 'Which I have been, but I'm still none the wiser.' Madison gave a tired laugh. 'To save myself from possible pain in the future, I'm inflicting a massive dose now.'

'So the treatment's worse than the cure?' Kerry smiled and Madison stared back, her mouth opening slightly to argue but realizing that she didn't have an answer!

'You know what? I dumped my fiancé this weekend.' Suddenly Kerry didn't look so much the confident professional she portrayed so well. In fact, on closer inspection her well-made-up eyes revealed puffiness, and despite the porcelain powdered complexion her nose was just a touch red. Madison stood dangling her bag in her hand as Kerry went on. 'On paper he was perfect. He had every attribute I could list in a man, there was nothing about him I could really object to—he was supportive, funny, good-looking and educated…'

'But?' Madison gave a sympathetic smile as she rummaged in her bag for her cheque book.

'That's what I'm trying to work out,' Kerry admitted, waving her hand as Madison started to write out a cheque. 'Why, when it looked so perfect on paper, didn't it feel quite so good in real life?'

'Here.' Tearing out the cheque, Madison went to hand it over, but Kerry waved it away.

'This one's on me.'

'You're sure?' Madison checked. 'I'm more than happy to pay.'

'I know you are but, yes, I'm sure.' Kerry nodded. 'I assume you don't want to make another appointment on your way out?'

'No.' Madison shook her head. 'But thank you, Kerry, thank you for all your help.'

'Good luck,' Kerry called as Madison stepped out of the office, and out into the early afternoon sun, blinking at a world that seemed brighter all of a sudden. Madison finally admitted why—Guy. Though initially she had been appalled, their love-making had been an utter revelation, a complete awakening, the side of her she'd suppressed for so very long, the impulsive, fun-loving Madison that had been buried with her husband. Walking the short distance back to the hospital, for the first time in years she wasn't rushing, merely walking; for the first time in a long time she literally stopped to smell the roses, to take stock of all she had and all she'd achieved…

To bravely face the future.

'We've got a problem!' Annie, the permanently frazzled ward clerk, jumped up from her desk as Madison slipped off her jacket. 'Beth's son, Jackson, is being brought in by ambulance. Apparently he's had a severe asthma attack at school. It sounds pretty bad.'

'Poor Beth.' Madison grimaced. 'OK, Beth knows, I assume?'

'Guy's talking to her now, getting Jackson's history and everything.'

'Good,' Madison said crisply. 'OK, who's the nurse in Resus…' Her voice trailed off as she realised the predicament. Beth Anderson was the most senior staff member on duty that afternoon and she was in charge of Resus. Annie nodded as the problem dawned.

'I'll go into Resus.'

'But you've got a full diary,' Annie pointed out. 'An

occupational health and safety lecture in fifteen minutes and then there's a management meeting to attend at two. Alanna's already said that she can take over Resus, so long as we can get an agency nurse to fill the gap. I just need you to sign off on it.'

'I'll go into Resus,' Madison said again, more firmly this time. 'Beth deserves the most senior staff available to look after her son.'

'Only you're not available,' Annie pointed out, running to keep up with Madison who was marching through the department. 'What do I tell everyone?'

'Tell them that something more important came up,' Madison responded. 'Tell them that I'm needed down here in the real world.'

'Right.' Madison nodded to Alanna. 'Have you alerted the paediatricians and anaesthetist?'

'I've just put out a page.' Alanna nodded.

'Well done. OK, Alanna, I'm going to take over in here, you carry on with the cubicles.'

'I am capable of running Resus,' Alanna said, a distinctly brittle edge to her voice, which, despite the critical time factor, Madison chose not to ignore, pulling out the red crash cart and pulling up drugs as she spoke.

'I don't doubt that for a moment but the fact is, Beth is the nurse down for Resus this afternoon, and clearly she can't be expected to run her own son's resuscitation. Now, given that you're up to date on what's happening out there, it makes far more sense for you to carry on and I'll pick up in here, rather than spending what little time we have before Jackson arrives trying to bring me up to speed. Annie's clearing my diary for the afternoon, but if I need a hand, I'll call.'

Only slightly mollified, Alanna gave a reluctant nod and walked out. Madison didn't dwell on it, her only thought right now for the seven-year-old boy coming in. She saw the flash of blue lights and heard the skid of brakes and a final wail of a siren that heralded the arrival of Jackson. Madison knew it was indeed serious. Blue lights and sirens on the streets were to alert traffic to move out of the way, but when they were used in the hospital driveway it was for the opposite reason, to alert people that help was needed, to move in close and try to save a life.

'Jackson Anderson,' a paramedic gasped as they skidded to a halt with the stretcher. Guy raced in alongside them, with a distraught Beth trying to hold herself back but desperate to get near. 'Seven-year-old, chronic asthmatic. Became breathless in the classroom and deteriorated quickly, semi-conscious on our arrival, tachypnoeic, using accessory muscles, with tracheal tug. His oxygen saturations were eighty-two per cent on our arrival and have come up to ninety per cent on oxygen and continued Ventolin nebuliser. He's been cannulated…'

All this was said as the little boy was swiftly moved over, his dark eyes rolling as Madison leant him forward, resting his frame on a large pad—upright being the best position, the most comfortable during an asthmatic episode to allow for greater lung expansion. But Jackson was too weak to support himself and Madison supported him with pillows as another nurse attached him to the monitors and connected the oxygen tube to the hospital supply, sharing a brief anxious look with the paramedics.

'Thanks, Ben,' Madison said. 'Good job.'

'We'll grab a cuppa,' Ben said, which might have sounded a strange thing to say, but everyone present knew it had nothing to do with a brew and everything to do with hanging around to find out what was going to happen to the little boy, who was working so hard simply to breathe.

'This is more like a massive anaphylactic reaction,' Guy said, listening to Jackson's chest, then probing his neck with his fingers. 'Beth said he had a nut allergy…'

'He wouldn't eat nuts,' Beth shouted. 'He doesn't eat anything that I don't give him.'

'Let's lay him flat and get some adrenaline into him,' Guy said, ignoring Beth for now, his only focus on the patient, a steady hand taking the drugs Madison handed to him. She could only marvel at his cool. A child as sick as this meant a tense resuscitation room, especially given the fact it was a staff member's child and that she was present.

'Do you want Beth to leave?' Madison asked, turning her eyes to the saturation monitor. The percentages were dropping ominously as Jackson's heart rate accelerated, his tiny heart working overtime to drag vital oxygen in and failing, his lungs too rigid to allow for any air expansion.

'Let her stay for now,' Guy replied. 'Where are the paediatricians?'

'On their way,' Jane answered. 'I've just put out an urgent call for the anaesthetist.'

'Beth.' Guy looked up briefly. 'I'm going to intubate Jackson. His saturations are dropping, we need to do this. Do you want to stay or go?'

Beth opened her mouth to argue, no doubt to insist that this couldn't be happening, that her child didn't need such drastic measures, that her baby wasn't at death's door, but somehow she held back and summoned the strength to resist holding her child, in her eyes a desperate plea for help as she nodded her consent to Guy and handed her trust over to him.

'Stay, I want to stay…'

'Hold his hand,' Guy responded, nodding to the staff to make room for her. 'Talk to him, Beth, tell him he's going to be OK.'

But was he?

Jackson's blood pressure was dangerously low, his oxygen saturations rapidly diminishing, his body collapsing. His respiration rate, which had been so high in an exhausting attempt to get vital oxygen, was now starting to decrease. Even his heart rate was slowing, and Madison knew that Guy couldn't wait for an anaesthetist. If they didn't intubate Jackson now, they would lose him.

Guy's hand was amazingly steady, just one impatient curse as he attempted to put the tube into the boy's spasmed throat, and failed. Madison found she was holding her own breath as Guy steadied himself, forced himself to focus, to ignore the machines bleeping behind him, to drown out Beth's frantic loving words to her son and concentrate on the vital task in hand.

'I'm in.' He held the tube very still as Madison secured it carefully, making sure they didn't move the vital connection, then Madison took over, bagging the little boy as Guy listened to his chest, making sure the airway was indeed in the right place, giving a relieved nod when he heard the breath sounds.

'Poor air entry…'

Madison didn't need to point out that at least he *had* some air entry now. The last few seconds before Guy had intubated Jackson had really been dire and Madison stood watching as the oxygen saturations that had been dipping into the high fifties started to lift, into the seventies then eighties, reaching a plateau around ninety per cent, which wasn't great but was certainly much better than they'd had.

'I want an adrenaline infusion,' Guy said, not stopping when the paediatrician raced in, giving out orders. He had control, the patient still too critical to allow for a handover. The paediatric team respected that, listening intently as Madison filled them in while Guy worked on. But slowly he started handing over the reins when the situation allowed, discussing latest treatments and protocols, checking on the intensive care situation, working with the paediatricians and anaesthetist to stabilise this little life, until finally Beth had the confidence to leave him for a few moments, to go to the interview room and make an endless round of phone calls to let her family know what had taken place.

'There's no ICU beds, Mark.' Madison came off the phone from the supervisor and addressed the paediatrician. 'The one they did have has just been taken by a surgical patient. They're extubating a patient in the next couple of hours so there's a chance there could be one by evening…'

'Or someone could die,' Guy added. The appalling, hopeless irony hit its mark and Madison gave a weary smile.

'There's always that chance, I guess.'

'He needs good intensive care.' Mark tapped his pen against his thigh as he looked at the little boy. 'I'm not saying that he won't get that down here—'

'I know you're not,' Madison broke in. 'But there's a very good chance that the ICU patient they're talking about extubating won't be up to being transferred and, as Guy pointed out, unless someone dies there's not going to be an intensive care bed. Frankly, Mark, I don't have the staff to special one patient for an indefinite period. Who knows what's about to come through the doors? I've already rung the children's hospital and told them the situation. They're happy to take him, they can arrange for the paediatric emergency transfer team to collect him, but they need a doctor to give the go-ahead.'

'Do you think I should ask for a helicopter or ambulance?' Mark asked.

Madison glanced down at her watch. It was already nudging two forty-five and by the time the team were mobilized, it would be another hour before they arrived. The paediatric emergency transfer team was highly skilled and organized, and they would take their time to get a good handover from the paediatrician and ensure Jackson was as stable as possible before the journey. So even though their response would be rapid, the actual retrieval would take some time and rush-hour traffic, combined with a critically ill child, wasn't an ideal situation even if they were heading in the opposite direction to the peak-hour cars.

'Helicopter,' Madison said, and Mark nodded, heading out to pick up where Madison had left off.

'Amazing!' Guy said, shaking his head in disbelief then saying it again. 'Amazing.'

'What is?' Madison asked. She checked Jackson's obs and popped a fresh sheet over him and a small flat pillow under his head to make him look more comfortable before Beth came back in. But unlike most doctors, Guy unfolded the sheet with Madison from the other side of the bed, picking up a few discarded wrappers and generally tidying up with her as they chatted. Even though they were both avoiding each other's eyes, both clearly a touch uncomfortable, they pushed aside all that happened yesterday—a patient's bedside, even if he was unconscious, not the place to discuss what had taken place. Madison was grateful for the small reprieve.

'Helicopter or ambulance! It just rolls off your tongue. I still can't get used to it—hell, I still can't get used to having a choice of antibiotics, a phone I can pick up and have any number of specialists racing down to assist.'

'But are you enjoying it?' Madison asked. It sounded like a stupid question but, being used to Emergency, she knew that as angst-ridden as his relief work might have been, in many ways Guy would have enjoyed the autonomy, the chance to make a very real difference in the most dire of circumstances. And he had done that over and over—from the tiny glimpses he had revealed, Madison knew that Guy had witnessed many things.

'Actually, I am enjoying it,' Guy said. 'And I have to admit it's come as a pleasant surprise. Since I was in England I haven't worked in an actual structured health system, and I thought I'd be wringing my hands at the injustice of it all. But instead I'm just glad to finally be in a well-stocked, well-run hospital and able to use my brain.'

'I'm sure you used your brain before,' Madison rebuked. 'As you said, you had no back-up.'

'To tell you the truth, I felt more like an odd-job man at times, making do with this, trying out that. I've made hundreds of IV splints out of bits of wood, incubators with a couple of light globes and a rattly old generator. It's a bit of a novelty asking for something and actually getting it!' He stared down at Jackson, sedated and with a tube down his throat, lines and monitors everywhere. But his obs were more stable and there was a hint of colour in a face that had been way too pale. Guy brushed back the damp, sweaty hair from his forehead. 'You might not realize it, Jackson, but you're a very lucky boy.

'I'd better go and speak to Beth and tell her about the transfer.'

'And I'd better hand over Jackson to the late shift, it's nearly time for me to go home.'

By the time Madison had spoken again with the transfer team, liaised with Mark and handed Jackson over to the late shift nurse who was covering the resuscitation room, Guy was back. 'How's Beth?' Madison asked as she pulled on her jacket and handed over the drug keys and pager to her replacement.

'Not great,' Guy admitted. 'From what Beth told me, she's really struggled to let go a bit. His asthma and allergies have been difficult to control and it took a lot for her to send him to school, to let him go to parties—this isn't going to help. I've told her that, given the severity of his reaction, Jackson's going to have to carry adrenaline now, and that his carers will be trained to administer it, but at the end of the day I can't blame her one bit for not wanting to ever let him out of her sight again. I can't believe the school let this happen.'

'Oh, come on, Guy,' Madison said. Information had started to trickle in and a child sitting next to Jackson had been eating peanut butter sandwiches. 'We know how sever a genuine nut allergy can be, but most people don't. Can you imagine how awful the school is feeling right now, how that poor mum who made her kid's lunch today is going to feel when she finds out that the sandwiches she made nearly killed another child?'

'I guess.' Guy gave a weary smile. 'That's one kid who won't be having peanut butter ever again.'

'Two.' Madison grinned. 'At least Emily won't be

having it in her lunchbox at school any more. Anyway, I'd better go.'

'Me, too,' Guy said, smothering a yawn. 'I've had enough of this place for a week.'

As she turned to go Guy called her back. 'Can I walk out with you?'

And even though her back was to him Madison knew that, like her, he was holding his breath. Turning slowly, she nodded, taking the biggest, bravest step of her life. 'I'd like that.'

Of course it was never that easy. Guy had a list of things he had to do, a couple of quick phone calls to make and a chart to sign off, and the most obvious thing in the world would have been for Madison to just walk off. It was the only thing she'd have done just a day ago, but today she found herself waiting, a tiny bit embarrassed perhaps but waiting all the same. Eventually they walked through the department and out into the car park.

'How did you do with your life coach?' Guy asked, a tiny teasing ring to his voice.

'I sacked her,' Madison responded, smiling at his rather shocked response. 'Well, when I say I sacked her, we amicably agreed that perhaps we'd run our course.'

'Madison…' Guy started, but Madison just shook her head.

'It was nothing you said, Guy. The simple truth of the matter is that for a while there it worked for me. I needed someone to guide me through the jumble my life was in and Kerry fitted the bill—cool detachment and an objective opinion was exactly what I needed for a while.'

'And now?' When Madison didn't answer, Guy spoke for her, gave her another question to dwell on. 'How about I come over tonight? Just to talk, Madison. We kind of left things in the air yesterday.'

'I'd like that,' Madison was amazed to find herself admitting, amazed that she had actually managed to say it! 'Only I'm babysitting for my friend tonight.'

'Tomorrow night, then?'

'Same again.' Madison winced. 'I owe Helen a lot of favours after this week. I don't usually rely so heavily on her. Anyway, I'm not sure it's a good idea, you coming to the house. I don't want Emily to think…' Her voice trailed off. How could she explain to a man as footloose and fancy-free as Guy the drama that could ensue from a simple dinner date, that the last thing she wanted to do was expose Emily to even a hint that she was dating, until Madison was sure that she really was dating, so to speak? But how on earth was she supposed to start dating without being able to accept a casual dinner invitation?

'I could bring a briefcase,' Guy offered, smiling as it became clear that Madison had no idea what he was on about. 'In fact, there are a few things I'd like to go over with you, given that I'm taking over from Gerard. A business dinner.' Guy grinned as Madison blinked back at him. 'A colleague dropping over for a chat, and he just happens to be bringing some Chinese food with him, maybe even a nice bottle of wine.'

'But we can't. I mean, there can't be any repeats...' Madison swallowed hard, knowing that, as Emily and Richard were going to be there, she had to make this absolutely clear, but blushing to her roots as she did so. 'We can't do anything.'

'You mean, we can't rip our clothes off and do it on your lounge room floor again?' Guy asked, somehow managing to keep a straight fact as Madison's cheeks turned purple. But despite her embarrassment, she was glad it was out in the open, grateful to him for bringing it up, joking about it even.

'No,' Madison managed, fumbling in her bag for her keys and wrenching her car door open, desperate for the relief of the stuffy confines of a car that had been in the sun all day, as opposed to the hothouse of emotions Guy was stirring up. 'And,' she added, winding down her window, marginally safer now there was a metal door between them, 'I actually prefer Thai food.'

CHAPTER SIX

'THANK you so much for this.' Helen accepted a glass of wine from Madison with a shaking hand. 'You have no idea how nervous I am.'

'Well, you look stunning,' Madison reassured her friend, and every word was genuine. Helen's pale blonde hair had been beautifully trimmed and blow-dried, her face was gently made up and the permanent jeans and T-shirt had been replaced with a simple black dress. 'You've got legs!' Madison winked.

'I've got very smooth legs,' Helen corrected. 'And painted toenails. I wish I could stop shaking for five minutes. He's going to think I've got alcohol with-drawal or something. I'm a nervous wreck!'

'But what have you got to be nervous about? He's only taking you to dinner—you can talk under water at the best of times.'

'It's the fourth course I'm worried about,' Helen moaned. 'You know that horrible bit, where you decide whether or not to ask him in for coffee. I feel like a vir-gin on her wedding night, worse even! I'd have no idea what to do if I actually found myself naked and alone with a man. It's been so long!'

'Helen!'

Helen grinned. 'I'm hardly going to sleep with him on our first date. What sort of girl do you take me for!' She was too busy with her own problems to notice Madison's flaming cheeks, and anyway, Madison consoled herself as she wiped the kitchen bench for the hundredth time, it would never enter Helen's head that Madison could behave in such a way. She could tell her the truth right here and now and Helen simply wouldn't believe the wild passionate sex that Madison had indulged in so recently. Berating herself for the umpteenth time for her actions yesterday, appalled at her behaviour, Madison was curiously excited all the same, thrilled at the tiny glimpse of not Madison the nurse or mum or widow but Madison the woman.

'Not that I don't want to do anything…' Helen carried on, completely unaware that she'd lost her audience. 'It's just— Oh, I don't know. I want him to want me, but I don't want him to do anything about it yet. I just want to know that he wants to. Does that make sense?' She was so wrapped up in her own dilemma she didn't even notice that Madison didn't answer. 'It's just so hard the second time around. I never thought I'd be shaving my entire body again just to go out for dinner, or washing behind my ears just in case he decides to lick them.' She let out a loud laugh that had Madison snapping back to attention. 'Not that I want them to be licked, but you never know!'

'Licked?' Madison asked, desperately trying to appear as if she had been listening and aware she was failing miserably.

'I just want to be prepared for any eventuality.' Helen shrugged at Madison's bemusement. 'Anyway, enough about me. I've hired a couple of DVDs for the kids so hopefully you won't hear a peep out of them.'

'They'll be fine,' Madison assured Helen, still trying to work out what she had missed. 'Anyway, I've got a colleague coming over from the hospital to go over a few things…'

'Who?' Helen asked idly, taking a sip of her wine. And then, for the first time since she'd arrived, her mind moved from her impending date and she actually looked at Madison, a slow smile breaking out on her face. 'Wow—look at you!'

'What?' Madison shuffled uncomfortably. 'I'm wearing shorts and a T-shirt.'

'Oh, but there's shorts and a T-shirt and then there's shorts and a T-shirt! You look amazing.'

Not quite amazing, Madison thought, but she was pleased with her appearance tonight. Her newly washed hair hung in a sleek heavy mass, thanks to some horribly expensive conditioner and, like Helen, her smooth legs glowed with body lotion. Her outfit consisted of a pair of smart, coffee-coloured, tailored shorts and a scoop-necked tight T-shirt, just the softest of soft leather belts providing a contrast. Her newly painted coral toenails peeped through her very new sandals.

'I assume it isn't Shirley, the nursing supervisor,

coming over to discuss a few things with you,' Helen teased lightly.

'No.' Madison shrugged, picking up a dishcloth and scrubbing the bench again.

'Or Alanna—the wannabe NUM?'

'No.'

'Then who on earth could it be?' Helen frowned then her face broke into a wicked smile. 'It couldn't be the dashing new consultant, could it?' Helen teased, her lips twitching wider as Madison tensed. 'The one who looks as if he's just rolled out of bed?'

'Yes, in fact, it is Guy that happens to be coming over, but it's just to discuss a few things. Now that he's the acting director he needs to come up to speed with what Gerard was implementing. There's a lot to discuss and at work whenever we try to talk, one of us invariably gets called away. It's no big deal so, please, don't make it one.'

'Whatever you say, Madison.' Helen grinned and gave her a saucy wink. 'Right, I'm off to meet my Friday night date. I've told Richard that I'm going out with an old friend from school, just in case he asks. You enjoy your business dinner.'

It would have been so easy to make Helen squirm in return, to tell her that not only did Emily and Richard know exactly where she was off to tonight, but no doubt so did half the school. But Madison simply didn't have the heart to deliver payback so instead she followed Helen along the hallway.

'Good luck,' Madison called, once Helen had kissed

Richard goodnight and was walking down the garden path towards her own house. 'Helen?'

She watched her friend turn around but instead of saying what was on her mind, instead of asking her if she was mad to be having Guy over, if she was making the most stupid mistake of her life, Madison just gave another wave to her friend. But they'd been through too much together for Helen not to be able to read her mind.

'Good luck, Madison,' Helen called. 'You'll be fine.'

Helen had actually been right.

Fraught with nerves, Madison answered the door in a blind panic, wondering what on earth she'd agreed to, what on earth they were going to talk about, how Emily was going to react to a strange man in the house. Appalling scenarios raced through her head, but they were quelled almost instantly. Guy, relaxed and casual in jeans and a T-shirt, had brought enough food to feed an army, which gave Madison a chance to utilise her trembling hands, by laying the table and pulling the goodies out of the brown paper bags. Emily wandered in with a curious look on her face, followed by Richard.

'Hello!' Suspiciously she eyed Guy. 'Who are you?'

'My name's Guy,' he said. 'I'm a doctor from the hospital. You must be Emily.' When she didn't answer, just stood with her hands on her hips staring boldly at him, Guy explained further. 'I've got a few things to talk over with your mum.'

'About the hospital?' Emily asked, rolling her eyes.

'Yep.' Guy nodded. 'I brought some dinner as well. Do you want some?'

'Yuck,' Emily responded as Madison scooped out some Thai green curry. 'I don't like anything that smells.'

'That rules out a lot of food.' Guy grinned. 'You really don't like anything that smells?'

'Well, I guess I like tuna,' Emily ventured, and Madison watched as a gap-toothed smile appeared on her face. 'And that stinks!'

'Yeah, but it's brain food,' Guy answered easily. 'If it makes you clever, I guess you can forgive it for smelling. Are you sure you don't want to try some of the curry?'

And Madison watched, opened-mouthed, as Emily wandered over, picked up a fork and dipped it into the food, twirling the noodles around and closing her eyes as she tasted it.

'It's…' Her five-year-old dictionary didn't quite have the capacity to give a detailed description, but actions spoke louder than words when her fork dipped back to the plate and scooped up another mouthful. 'It's really nice,' she finally agreed. 'Smelly but nice—and it burns your tongue even after you've swallowed it! I'm full now but can we get it some night, Mum?'

'Sure,' Madison answered, but her throat had gone dry and she wished she had a daughter who adored nuggets and chips or burgers with extra cheese—not a five-year-old who actually liked Thai green curry.

'Come on, Em,' Richard called, obviously appalled

at the prospect of sitting down with two oldies and eating such disgusting food. 'The movie's about to start.'

'You're watching a movie?' Guy asked. 'Then you'll need this—even if you are full!' He held out a bag and Madison watched as Emily took it and opened it. She grinned and showed the contents to Richard, who in a nano-second revised his opinion of Guy, meeting his palm with a deft 'high five' then scuttling back to the lounge room.

'Popcorn?' Madison smiled, pouring out two glasses of wine and heading for the table. 'Any five-year-old would sell their soul for it.'

'I hope you don't mind.'

'Of course not.'

The food was delicious and the talk came surprisingly easily. They chatted about work at first, gossiping about their fellow colleagues until finally, when the plates had been cleared and the kids were on their second movie, Madison found the courage to say what was on her mind.

'About yesterday…'

'Please, don't apologise,' Guy said. 'Please, don't cheapen it.'

'I'm not sorry.' Boldly she stared back at him, taking in the evident surprise on his face at her reaction. 'I'm embarrassed, mortified, stunned that I gave in so easily…'

'Please, don't feel bad about it. I know it was probably completely out of character for you, but if it's any consolation, it was for me as well.'

'Really?' Madison raised a questioning eyebrow. 'I would have thought there would have been a few nurses to fill those long lonely nights under a mosquito net.'

'Really,' Guy insisted. 'You can forget the romantic image you've got of my life. Generally there's no running water, so by the end of a long hot day and a few weeks without a shower, getting up close and personal isn't exactly at the top of anyone's agenda. The work's so damn exhausting that by the time you've patched up the holes in the mosquito net all you want to do is sleep. I've had a couple of romances along the way, but I can assure you, Madison, that AID work isn't some sort of extended, boozy, singles holiday club!'

'I know.' Suitably chastised, Madison gave a small shrug. 'The thing is,' Madison said slowly, running a nervous finger around her wineglass, 'I think I may have misled you, made you think that I was on the lookout for some sort of relationship.'

'I was very happy to be misled.' Guy grinned, but his voice grew serious when it became clear Madison had something important to say. Checking that the kids were settled, Madison closed the living-room door before joining him back at the kitchen table.

'When people find out that you're a widow, they assume that you had a happy marriage and you're suddenly exalted to almost a nun-like status. The fact of the matter is that I don't feel guilty about yesterday because of some misguided loyalty to Mark—that's my late husband,' she added, and Guy nodded his understanding. 'Mark and I were having some very serious problems.

I fell head over heels in love with him the day I met him. My parents warned me about him, said that he was irresponsible, that he couldn't be relied on, but I didn't listen. We were married within six months of meeting and the next thing I knew I was pregnant.'

Madison took a deep breath. 'Then I realized that my parents had been right all along. Mark was completely irresponsible. He adored Emily, but he certainly didn't let her stifle him. He still went away with his friends, still blew a small fortune on motorbikes and holidays, and goodness knows what else. Two days before he died I'd decided to leave him. When he was killed, it turned out that he'd "forgotten" to pay insurance for his bike, had "forgotten" to take out life insurance and "forgotten" to tell me that he'd forged my signature to remortgage the house.'

'Oh, Madison.' Instinctively he reached out and took her hand, but as right as it felt, as much as she needed comfort now, mindful of Emily, Madison pulled her hand away, fiddling instead with her hair, winding a newly washed lock round and round one finger as she relived the bleakest time of her life.

'It's taken me years to get my life together, to build a secure home for Emily. That's why I've been seeing Kerry—the life coach. She's helped me get my career moving, helped me finally get my finances in order. I never want to be in that sort of position again. I'm actually not a materialistic person. When I was married to Mark I was impulsive and spontaneous, but look where it got me.'

'You've done well,' Guy said softly. 'You've got a friendly, welcoming home, and even though I've only met her briefly, Emily seems incredibly together and confident.'

'She is,' Madison said fondly. 'The thing is, she's also very like her father and sometimes I get scared for her.'

'Why?'

'That she's going to be nightmare as a teenager, that she'll suddenly quit school and get her eyebrow pierced, or, worse still, decide to join a bikie gang…' She looked up as Guy did the most inappropriate thing—laughed at her fears. But it was totally without malice and Madison found herself smiling too and finally laughing, the fears that haunted her almost disappearing now that she'd voiced them.

'She's a little girl,' Guy said, topping up her wine-glass. 'You've got a good few years before you have to start worrying about that type of thing. Anyway, she's got you to guide her.'

'I know,' Madison admitted.

'Do you also know that most parents worry about that type of thing?'

'I guess,' Madison admitted.

'Though not where I've been lately,' Guy said. 'There aren't too many motorbike gangs and body-piercing salons. Still,' he added, his voice serious now, 'they have their own very real fears to deal with, their own concerns for their children growing up, and it's not just about where their next meal's going to come from.

They do have the problem of their kids being led astray, falling into the wrong company. Believe me, ten-year-olds with guns are a reality in some places.'

'Gosh.' Madison blinked, appalled at the thought, half-forgotten news articles coming to mind. 'At least that's one thing I don't have to worry about.'

'There's one thing you should be worrying about, though,' Guy said gently, and Madison screwed her eyes closed, knowing what was coming next. 'Yourself.'

'I'm fine.'

'When was the last time you had a night out?' Guy asked. 'When was the last time you dressed up and went out for dinner?'

'Emily and I often—' Madison started, then clamped her mouth closed.

'When was the last time you went out—?'

'I'm not ready for dating,' Madison snapped, but when Guy carried on talking she realized he hadn't even scratched the surface.

'If you'd let me finish, I was going to ask when the last time was you went out to see a movie that wasn't an animated kids' one.' Madison pursed her lips as he pushed on. 'When was the last time you went out for a night with the girls or even for a coffee with a friend?'

'Ages,' Madison admitted. 'I've actually decided to make a bit more of an effort on that front. I'm going to make some time for me, find a reliable babysitter and start going out a bit. I'm finally starting to realize that I do need a bit more adult company—away from work.'

'Good.' Guy smiled. 'And is there any chance of me

being a part of that adult company?' When she opened her mouth to speak he overrode her. 'Can I take you out for dinner at least—once you find that reliable babysitter?'

'I was talking about female company, Guy.' Madison swallowed. 'Getting a social life going was what I meant, perhaps joining a book club or something—not dating. The last thing I need right now is a relationship. I'm just not prepared to let anyone jeopardise what I've fought so hard to build.'

'Maybe things wouldn't be jeopardised,' Guy said gently. 'It could even enhance things, make things better.'

Madison shrugged. 'I'm not prepared to chance it, Guy. At the end of the day I've got a five-year-old daughter, and I know it's way too soon to be looking ahead, but that's how it has to be when you've got a child—at least, that's how I feel.'

'So you're never going to go out with a man again.'

'Not for the foreseeable future,' Madison answered, ignoring the incredulous edge to his voice and deliberately keeping hers even. 'I can't just date freely, bring different men into Emily's life until I meet the right one. I simply won't do that to her.'

'What if you've already met him?' Guy asked. Madison gave him a startled look, shocked yet relieved at the depth of feeling behind his words, scarcely able to comprehend that Guy could be feeling this as much as her. 'Look, I can't rationalise what's taken place. The truth of the matter is if I wrote up one of your blessed lists and put down what I was looking for in a woman, a single mum with a tendency to obsessive compulsive disorder wouldn't be at the top of it, but…' He gave a helpless shrug. 'I didn't mean it to come out like that.'

'Don't worry.' Madison gave a dry laugh. 'A perpetual backpacker isn't exactly at the top of my list either. Do you see now why we can't take this further?'

'No,' Guy answered, smiling at her frown. 'I can see why we have to take things very slowly. I can see why it would be a very good idea if I go home now and not try and rush things. Are you free at any time tomorrow?'

'Emily has a dance lesson,' Madison answered unthinking. 'At nine a.m.'

'So how about we do breakfast?' Guy suggested. 'You can tell Emily that you're going shopping—she doesn't even have to know. You name the place.'

He made it sound so easy, so straightforward, and Madison found herself being swayed.

'We'll take things so slowly Emily won't even know I'm around. We can have lunch at work, the odd dinner when you can get a babysitter. Breakfast once a week would be a good starting point.'

'Just breakfast?'

'Emily won't even know we've met.'

She was touched more than she could say that he would leave now when he clearly wanted to stay, that he would meet her for a mere hour and a half just to talk with her, just to spend time with her. Madison found herself nodding, not just about tomorrow but at the possibility he was offering, that maybe they could make this work. Maybe he was a man she could actually trust.

'There's a nice café on the high street,' Madison gulped. 'I could get there about five past nine.'

'It's a date, then,' Guy said, standing up and heading for the front door. But as they walked past the living room, when he was sure the door was closed, he pulled her into his arms, dusted her forehead with his lips, melting away the tension that was there. Then his mouth found hers and he silenced the questions that were there with the briefest but most tender of kisses, before reluctantly letting her go and heading off into the night.

And yesterday faded almost into insignificance—yes, the sex had been amazing, reckless and exciting, but the tiny kiss they had just shared had spun her into orbit. The depth and emotion behind it, the glimpse of promise within it, had her senses reeling. Her fingers came to her lips, pushing the flesh beneath them as if somehow he were still there, tasting him all over again then snapping out of her daydream as Emily bustled out of the living room.

'Where's Guy?' Emily asked, holding out a bowl. 'I was going to see if he wanted some popcorn.'

'He's gone home, honey.' Madison smiled. 'And I think it's time you two went to bed.'

'Five more minutes.' Emily pouted. 'We won't make a noise.'

'Five minutes, then,' Madison agreed, but as Emily headed off to the living room she paused, her shrewd eyes turning back to Madison, her pretty face way too knowing for her years.

'I like Guy,' she said to Madison, staring directly at her mother. 'And I think that you like him, too.'

CHAPTER SEVEN

'BUT where are you going?' Emily asked, unaccustomed to any change in their strict routine. 'You always watch me dance.'

'I know, darling, but today I need to go shopping. I'll be back at ten-thirty…' A knot of anxiety tightened in her stomach and she decided that if Emily got upset and asked for her to stay, she'd ring Guy on his mobile and cancel. But Emily gave a tiny shrug and absent-mindedly kissed Madison goodbye before disappearing into a sea of pink-leotarded little girls. It was painfully obvious to Madison that Emily couldn't give two hoots about the change in her routine.

Painful because now she had absolutely no excuse not to go and meet Guy for breakfast.

'I was expecting a phone call.' Smiling as she nervously sat down in front of him, Guy placed his mobile on the table beside them. 'I was sure you were going to ring and cancel.'

'I was sure I was going to.' Madison smiled and accepted a menu from a busy waitress. 'In fact, I'm clearly nowhere near the perfect mother because I was praying Emily would burst into tears and beg me to stay.'

'She didn't?'

'No.' Madison shook her head. 'She barely managed to scrape together a kiss and a goodbye before she was off to be with her friends. I definitely need to improve my social life because my five-year-old's is already miles more active than mine.'

'What do you fancy?' Guy asked. 'Apart from that?'

'Guy!' Madison squealed, her cheeks bursting into colour as he read her mind. Refusing to look up till her colour had subsided, she scanned the menu. 'Pancakes, with maple syrup and bacon.'

'Madison Walsh!' Guy tutted. 'That's not very calorie-controlled of you.'

'I like my food.' Madison shrugged, but Guy just stared. 'What?'

'What about all those healthy meals for one I saw in your cupboard?'

'I have them because they're easy,' Madison said, surprised that he'd noticed. 'I'm hardly going to cook chicken tarragon with jasmine rice just for me, and Emily's a real meat-and-two-veg girl. It's certainly not a desire to be healthy, more a desire for taste, speed and convenience. You really think you've got me labeled, don't you?'

'Not a bit,' Guy answered thoughtfully. 'Every time I think I'm getting to know you, out pops another surprise. You're nothing like the woman I thought you were.'

'And what was she?'

'Uptight!' Guy grinned. 'Mind you, I fancied her like crazy.'

'And what am I now?' Madison asked, ignoring the second part of his statement but glowing inside.

'Uptight,' Guy said. 'But with a hell of a lot of potential. And, for the record I still fancy you like crazy.'

The food was delicious—at least, Madison assumed that the food was delicious because suddenly she was staring down at an empty plate. And the clocks must have changed last night and she'd forgotten, because an hour had disappeared in a flash, laughing, eating, exploring, getting to know each other, finding out all the silly little things that didn't really matter a scrap but mattered terribly at the start of a romance—that he took sugar in his coffee, that he rained salt and pepper on everything, that his star sign was Aries, and that his favourite indulgence after many years in the middle of nowhere was exactly the same as Madison's, a hot bath filled to the brim with bubbles...

'With a magazine,' Guy added. 'The trashier the better...' Seeing her stare regretfully at her watch, he halted the conversation and waved for the bill. 'Dance class over?'

'In ten minutes,' Madison replied, reaching for her purse. 'If I go now I can catch the last five minutes.'

'Let's go, then,' Guy said, completely ignoring the money she held out and paying the bill himself, before walking her outside. 'Would you like to do this again—

say, same time next week?' Guy asked, and Madison didn't even hesitate.

'Please.'

And it was the right answer, the right answer for both of them. A delighted Guy pulled her into his arms, his mouth crushing hers, the scratch of the brick wall behind her the only thing holding her up as she burnt under his touch like a teenager high on hormones. Oblivious to the throng of people in the high street, not even caring if half the parents at school were walking past, she kissed him back, felt the bruising weight of his lips on hers, until he pulled away, leaving her breathless and weak with longing, his touch so full of promise, affirming that a week between drinks, so to speak, was just too long to be without this divine man.

Nibbling her bottom lip, she gazed back up at him, dizzy with lust, trying to decide if she should take things further. Her mental scales carefully weighed up the pros and cons, carefully spooning on the utter joy that had filtered into her life during what should have been such a bleak time, adding the sensual, heady awakening he had so easily given her, topping it off with the sheer unadulterated pleasure of just being with him. She could feel the weight of his eyes on her, knew that he was waiting, hoping that she was going to move this forward yet refusing to coerce her, just patiently awaiting whatever came next.

But five years of pain couldn't be erased so easily. The scales that had seemed so heavily weighted in Guy's favour catapulted upwards as Mark's deception, his irresponsibility, the sheer hell he had inflicted shifted the balance as layer after layer of pain was scooped on and the scales teetered ominously against them. He must have seen the hurt in her eyes, felt the shift in her stance, because finally he spoke, dragging her back into his arms, but in a way that was more soothing than sexual, holding her close as her heart hammered against him, feeling her confusion and pain.

'There's no rush here, Madison,' Guy whispered in her ear, blocking out the busy sounds of people on the street, the Saturday morning traffic, until for all the world is was only the two of them. 'I'm not going anywhere.'

And it was exactly what she needed to hear, tiny grains of hope that shifted the balance back towards Guy, gave her the confidence she needed to face the possibility of a future with Guy beside her, to move things along just a shade more.

'Madison's going to Mark's parents on Wednesday night, she stays over once a month for a contact visit. Maybe you could come over, we could have dinner, I could cook…' And she felt him hold her tighter, his breath still in his lungs as she took the first brave step towards a future, invited him a touch further into her life.

'Leave the details to me,' Guy murmured. 'But there's no way you're cooking.' Reluctantly he let her go, but she left hastily, her mind whirring. Thrilled, terrified, excited by what she had done, she raced to the dance hall and arrived just as the class ended. She anxiously glanced through the window as she scuttled past and twenty little girls made curtsies.

Surely everyone must know, Madison thought, blushing scarlet as she waded through the throng of mothers towards Emily. Surely everyone had seen her kissing a stranger in the street, surely it was flashing like a neon sign above her head. But no one seemed to even look at her, no one even gave her a second glance as, dizzy and breathless, she found her daughter peeling off her ballet shoes then peeling off her wide pink hairband, a smile lighting up her face as she saw her mother—not remotely fazed by the fact that Madison was all of fifteen seconds late.

'Hi, Mum!' A tiny frown puckered her face as she stared back at her mother, and a million thoughts crashed into Madison's mind. She wondered for an appalling second if she really did have a neon sign flashing over her head or, more probably, whether her face was smeared with lipstick. 'What did you get?'

Madison gave her a helpless look.

'You haven't got any bags,' Emily pointed out. 'I thought you said that you were going shopping.'

'I've been window-shopping,' Madison offered, but Emily stared at her nonplussed.

'What's that?'

'Window-shopping,' Madison said again, waiting for the penny to drop, then realizing with a stab of pain that Emily would have no idea what she was talking about. That somewhere between getting her life structured and organized, somewhere between paying the mortgage and fighting to give her little girl what Madison had been sure she'd needed, somewhere along the way, probably right at the beginning, spontaneity had been lost and she'd somehow neglected to give what every child needed—a chance to just be.

'It's just for fun,' Madison explained. 'You don't actually buy anything, you just wander round the shops, looking.'

'Why?'

'Come on,' Madison said, mentally pushing aside the grocery shopping and the mad dash to get to the bank, which only opened for a few hours on Saturday morning, to race back home before the ice cream melted to an unsalvageable mess in the boot and then attempt to make a dent in the laundry that invariably piled up over the week. 'I'll show you.'

'But I'm in my ballet clothes.'

'So what?' Madison asked, and Emily blinked back at her mother, clearly shocked that her mother wasn't suggesting they race home and change, or pulling out a neatly folded T-shirt and skirt from her bag.

'So what?' Emily repeated, an excited smile breaking out on her face, Standing up, she took her mother's hand and they headed out to the street, ready to have some fun.

'That wasn't really window shopping,' Emily said, between blowing bubbles into her strawberry milkshake, sitting only two tables down in the café from where her mother had sat only a couple of hours before. 'Because we did buy something!'

Quite a few somethings, actually, Madison thought, feeling the weight of shopping bags around her ankles as she sipped on her very welcome cappuccino.

They were OK with money.

Not rolling in it, but not struggling either. The decision to keep Emily at the school she was happy at had been made now and it was as if a huge burden, both financial and emotional, had been lifted. No need to save every penny for a rainy day now. Of course, given what she had been through, Madison knew she would always be sensible, but now, finally, after all this time, she had the confidence to relax a touch—to stop worrying about potential rainy days and instead bathe in the delicious warm rays of the sun whenever it chose to shine—and it was shining now.

'We deserve it.' Madison grinned, thinking of her gorgeous sheer top and the most divine pair of shoes to ever have graced her feet nestling safely in their mounds of tissue paper.

'I love my fairy wings.' Emily giggled. 'Can I wear them to bed tonight?'

'I guess so,' Madison said, 'given that I'll be wearing my shoes!'

CHAPTER EIGHT

'Do you speak Sudanese?'

Only briefly knocking on his office door before she entered, Madison strode in.

'A tiny bit,' Guy answered, sensing the urgency in her voice and ignoring the chance for a smart comeback. 'Why?'

'A woman's presented to the maternity department. She's a new migrant to Australia, she's only been in the country for a couple of weeks. According to the records she's not pregnant. However…'

'How far?' Guy asked, getting straight to the point.

'Full term—at least they think so. They're trying to get an interpreter for her but they're not having much luck and it doesn't look as if they've got that much time to spare. She's got an old Caesarean scar and it's unclear whether that baby survived. Basically, they want to take her to Theatre, but they need someone to translate.'

'Fine. I'll go straight up.'

'You know we've got the budget meeting in an hour,'

Madison reminded him as Guy clicked off his pen and stood up.

'I'll tell the woman to hurry up and deliver, then,' Guy retorted, but softened it with a smile. 'I hate those meetings.'

'No, I'm the one who really hates those meetings,' Madison responded, but more to herself, rolling her eyes heavenwards at the thought of yet another meeting to discuss the findings of the last meeting. Glancing at her watch, Madison knew that if she wanted some lunch she'd better grab it now, but watching Guy head out the door, lunch was the last thing on her mind.

'Guy?' Madison called as he raced out the door, frowning as she halted him but briefly turning around. 'Can I come and watch?'

'Sure,' he said after only a beat of hesitation. 'So long as Maternity don't mind.'

The obstetrician and midwives didn't mind a bit. The relief on their faces when Guy appeared was evident. They barely even noticed Madison.

'Her name's Juka, and she doesn't like any equipment near her. All I've managed is to take a pulse and temperature. She won't even let me put the Doppler on to listen for the foetal heartbeat,' Moira, one of the midwives, explained. 'I tried to take her into the birthing suite and she panicked, so for now she's in her room. Brett, the on-call obstetrician, is in with her now, but from the sound of it he's not having any luck—basically the family just want to be left alone. She's got a classical Caesarean scar, and that's all we've been able to ascertain.'

A classical Caesarean scar was one that ran vertically down the abdomen and was rarely used now, except in the most dire of emergencies. The lateral incision was now the method of choice. Guy absorbed this information whole flicking through Juka's thin notes.

'She could have had a traumatic delivery in the past or it could have been just the method of choice at the time—but if she has had a bad time, that might explain why she's reluctant to be examined. Right, I'll go and see her. Seeing as you've met her, can you come in with me, Moira. If you don't mind, I'll bring in Madison as well. Someone has to account for my minutes spent away from the department after all, and who better than the NUM?'

'Sure.' Moira shrugged, but her answer came a beat too late. She was clearly wondering what good an emergency nurse could be, but Guy already had that one worked out.

'We work well together,' Guy explained, pulling on some gloves outside the room. 'I'm not the only one who could use a familiar face right now.'

Entering the darkened room, they were met by a rather fraught-looking obstetrician. 'The husband won't let me examine her.'

'Let me talk to him,' Guy said, making his way over and introducing himself to the tall man standing quietly in the corner, a suspicious look on his face as three more strangers entered the room. But as Guy swiftly introduced himself he visibly relaxed and talked rapidly to Guy as Moira and Madison turned their attention to Juka.

A statuesque, gracious-looking woman, she was leaning over the sink in the room. Her eyes were closed, but not tightly, and concentration was etched on every feature. But she was curiously relaxed, nodding gratefully as Moira gently but unobtrusively rubbed her lower back as Guy translated the conversation he was having.

'Juka has had two normal deliveries since the "operation."' Everyone present heard the quotation marks Guy carefully placed around the words. 'I think, and bear in mind my Sudanese is very basic, their first child died *in utero* and there were no drugs to facilitate a delivery so they operated, but the anaesthetic wasn't very successful…' Moira's eyes met Madison's, both women sharing an anguished look for what this family must have been through. Guy carried on talking to Juka's husband and at one point his hand instinctively reached over and gripped his shoulder before he addressed the rest of the medical personnel in the room.

'She got a nasty infection, was very ill and very depressed afterwards—and I don't think discussing this now is helping much. She doesn't want any help. She wants to deliver her baby herself.' Guy carried on translating as Juka's partner spoke, but suddenly it was Juka speaking, holding on to the sink and slowly squatting down. 'Baby is coming now.'

'Let's get her over to the delivery room,' Brett said, clearly wanting the safety of numbers and preferably lots of equipment.

'Leave her!' Moira ordered. She supported Juka's

shoulders, holding on to the woman as Juka did what she'd already done twice before, barely a murmur escaping her lips as she bore down.

'I'll get the delivery pack,' Brett offered, but again Moira shook her head.

'We've already got one,' she said, gesturing to the table. 'She's fine, Brett. Just stay quiet or leave.'

Brett stayed quiet—they all did, watching as, in almost silence, Juka bore down, with no pain relief, with no aid or intervention, in what must have been the most frightening of circumstances, in a new country where she didn't even speak the language. Somehow she blocked it all out and focused on the task in hand. After just a couple of dignified small groans, Madison watched in awe as Juka reached down and delivered her own baby, lifting her tiny child into the world, clutching him to her chest, stroking the tiny face. Only then did Moira intervene, grabbing a bunny rug and wrapping it around the babe as everyone waited for it to cry…

Guy made his way over and watched earnestly as Moira rubbed the tiny dark body more vigorously, not wanting to intrude but not wanting to stand back and do nothing as the seconds ticked on. Madison watched as Guy's fingers moved toward the red emergency pusher, hastily peeling the paper on the delivery pack and handing Moira the cord ties and scissors so she could cut the cord and if necessary dash the baby over to the nursery. Only Juka remained calm, stroking her baby all over. Moira did the same and suddenly the baby's face moved. The eyes blinked, a tiny mouth opened, limbs angrily flailed as the newborn dragged in its first breath.

'A wee boy.' Moira grinned, guiding Juka to the bed and wrapping the pair in blankets as the husband moved closer. 'Oh, would you look at the curls on him? That is one beautiful baby.'

Tears were streaming down Moira's cheeks and only then did Madison realize that she was crying, too. She'd seen many births before but never one as beautiful and as low key as this. Nature had unfolded completely as it should, and Moira was right—it was an absolutely beautiful baby. His skin was a touch lighter than his mother's, he had tiny black knots of curls on his head and the most gorgeous mouth, which searched furiously for food. His tiny, beautifully shaped head turned instinctively towards his mother, looking for security in a new unfamiliar world.

'Let's leave them,' Guy suggested. 'I mean us three,' he added to Moira, who wasn't going anywhere. 'I think Juka won't have any problem coping with delivering the placenta—given how easily she delivered the baby!'

'That's one long baby,' Moira said, clutching Juka's hand.

Juka was holding hers back, speaking words that Madison didn't understand, but she just knew from her gestures that Juka was thanking Moira for her help and understanding—for being there for her.

'We'll be off, Moira,' Guy said quietly. 'If you can't get an interpreter and need some help, call me any time. Switch can ring me at home tonight if needed, so pass that on to the evening staff. I'll call up this afternoon and talk to Juka and her husband anyway—I'd like to hear their story myself.'

'Me, too,' Moira said, staring down at baby and mother, clearly wondering what they must have been through. 'Thanks so much, you two, for coming down. Given her history, it would have been awful for her to have been rushed into Theatre or delivery.'

'That was wonderful,' Madison breathed as they headed off to Admin for the budget meeting.

'You really like nursing, don't you?'

'I love it,' Madison admitted.

'So what are you doing stuck in an office when all you want to be is out on the floor?' Guy asked.

Madison gave a reluctant sigh. 'Because of the hours—and the money,' Madison said. 'Although if I did shift work, the allowances would actually make up my pay.'

'So why don't you?' Guy asked. 'Alanna's hanging out for your job and you're hanging out for hers—why don't you both swap?'

'You make it sound so easy,' Madison said as they both stopped at the canteen to grab a couple of coffees from the machine to take to the meeting.

'It is that easy,' Guy said, filling a cup and handing it to her before punching in the numbers of his own choice. 'Lots of the nurses in Emergency have kids, and they manage to make it work.'

'Most of them have partners,' Madison replied, wrapping a serviette around the hot cup before they headed back up the corridor and to the meeting where neither wanted to be.

'So do you,' Guy said as they reached the door. Madison was grateful for the serviette as her coffee slopped over the edges of her cup. 'If you want one, that is.'

'It's too soon to be talking that way,' Madison said, flustered, but Guy was completely unfazed, staring calmly back at her.

'Is it? I know how I feel, Madison. I want all of you—and that isn't going to change.'

'I've got some very exciting news,' Terrence Hall, the CEO, stared down the table at the gathered staff and Madison tried to drag her mind to the meeting in hand, but she was acutely aware of Guy sitting next to her, thoroughly bored, his long legs stretched out under the desk as he doodled on a pad. The budget meeting for the emergency department was ticking into its second hour. Guy's words had sent her into an absolute spin—even if they hadn't exactly been a revelation. Madison knew how she felt—knew how Guy felt too—it had been hearing him affirm it that had sent her into overdrive.

He wanted to be let into her life—wanted more than he was having.

He wanted the responsibility of a partnership, wanted to get to know Emily, who was so much a part of her. And what had seemed an impossibility only days ago was now a probability. It had become more a question of when rather than if she introduced him to Emily as her partner.

'As you know,' Terrence continued, and Madison again attempted to switch off her personal life and concentrate on the professional. 'We've been trying to find the best way to honour Gerard Dalton's contribution to the department, and we're looking into some way to commemorate his name in the emergency unit. Madison, you suggested naming the resuscitation area after him.'

'It's just an idea,' Madison responded, interested in the meeting now that it had turned away from figures and back to people. 'Or perhaps we could call the observation ward the Dalton ward...'

'Well, I've penciled in a meeting next week to discuss that. However, Yvonne Dalton and her solicitor came to see me earlier this week...' Madison felt Guy's body stiffen. His interest, which had been waning, suddenly picked up and Madison looked over at him, watching his taut face as he listened to what Terrence had to say. 'Apparently, Gerard left provision in his will for the hospital to implement a scholarship programme in his name. It's up to Yvonne as to how that scholarship should be administered but, following Gerard's wishes, she's come up with an extremely exciting proposal. As we all know, Gerard was a huge advocate of global medicine, of health care for all, not just the affluent. Now, the proposal is that when we are advertising for the intern rotation, we will offer within their contracts a fully funded, six-month trip to a developing country to practice medicine. Yvonne is looking into several options as to where the resources are most needed, but this has huge implications. If we stagger the internships we can provide a full-time doctor and in turn we will attract far higher caliber doctors for the intern positions. I don't need to tell you all that it's not just a matter of attracting doctors in this day and age—it's keeping them. This way, there's a big incentive for them to complete their programme at this hospital—it's a win-win situation for both.

'It sounds wonderful,' Madison said, trying to take it all in. Terrence was right. Attracting and retaining doctors was a never-ending task, but with a scholarship such as this, there was a very real chance of Heatherton Hospital recruiting some of Australia's best medical minds, of Gerard's vision for a real centre of medical excellence coming to fruition. She gave a tiny pensive smile at Gerard's foresight, excited at the prospect of what lay ahead.

'Right.' Terrence clapped his hands. 'I'm actually meeting Yvonne to go over some details in ten minutes so let's wrap things up. The final item to discuss is the advertisement placed for a new director of Emergency. Naturally this has unsettled some of the staff, but I'd just like to point out that, as happy as we are with your performance, Guy, legally we have to advertise the position externally and go through an interview process. This has nothing to do with your performance, and everything to do with adhering to procedure. Guy, like everyone, has to formally apply for the position and be interviewed by a board…' He carried on talking and even though every word he said was extremely carefully scripted, everyone present knew that basically the interview process was a mere formality. Guy had done an amazing job in the short time he had been there, had stepped up to the position in the most trying of times and that, if he wanted it, the job was basically his.

If he wanted it. And from what he had said before, clearly he did.

Walking out of the meeting, Madison held herself back from catching up with Guy, determined not to let their relationship spill over into the workplace, to give anyone even the slightest hint of what was going on. But her own troubles, real or imagined, disappeared as she saw Yvonne sitting in the waiting room. In the last few weeks the weight had fallen off her. Her usually vibrant eyes looked exhausted, her hair, though well styled, was somehow lifeless. Without her beloved Gerard she looked lost, and naturally Madison made her way over to say hello to the woman.

'Yvonne.' Madison smiled warmly. 'How are you?'

'Getting there,' Yvonne said. 'Did Terrence tell you about the scholarship programme?'

'He did,' Madison replied. 'Yvonne, it sounds wonderful. So many people could potentially benefit. I can't get my head around it. How about you, Guy?' Madison asked as Guy came over.

'It's a marvelous idea, Yvonne. It's going to take a lot of work, though.'

'I'm more than prepared for that.' Yvonne nodded firmly. 'Gerard had actually worked on the idea for a couple of years. He was hoping to get it off the ground himself once the hospital was up and running. This is what he really wanted to do, more than anything.

'Actually…' Yvonne turned and faced Guy '…I was hoping to have a word with you before I go in and see Terrence.'

'Sure,' Guy said, but despite the ease of his reply Madison sensed the tension and something told her that it was time to leave.

'It was nice seeing you, Yvonne.'

'I'll be in touch.' Yvonne smiled. 'Perhaps I could call you some time. I know Gerard would have liked you to be personally involved.'

'I'd like that, too,' Madison answered. 'I'll look forward to hearing from you.' Then she took her cue and slipped quietly away.

There was nothing Madison would have liked more than to tell her staff about what had taken place in the meeting, but it wasn't her tale to tell so instead she bit her lip and said nothing about the exciting news and ploughed on with her work. But though the idea of the scholarship buzzed in her mind, it was Guy's desire to move things forward that had Madison working on pure adrenaline. Her decision finally made, all she wanted to do was talk to him, to tell him how she was feeling, but the busy department squashed any hope of a chat and Madison only caught up with him at the end of her day, tapping on his office door with her bag over her shoulder as she headed for home.

'Busy?' Madison asked.

'Snowed under.' He gestured to the mountain of paperwork in front of him. 'This is the bit I hate most.'

'Me, too.' Madison smiled but it didn't quite meet her eyes. A tiny frown puckered her brow as, instead of taking five minutes for a chat, Guy resumed writing.

'It's great news about the scholarship,' Madison ventured, trying to prolong things, reluctant to leave when she had so much to say. 'It's going to be fantastic for the department. I wonder how long it will take to get things up and running.'

'Yvonne seems pretty keen to get things moving, but nothing's going to happen overnight.' Guy shrugged. 'These things take for ever to get started. It could all amount to nothing.'

'I hope not,' Madison responded. 'There's no better way of honouring Gerard's memory. This is something he'd be so proud of.'

'Perhaps,' Guy said, fiddling with his pen and staring moodily at his work. Madison's frown deepened at his lack of enthusiasm.

'I'd better get home,' she said, her voice uncertain. She turned around and waited for him to call her back, for Guy to tell her whatever it was that was clearly on his mind. She consoled herself that he'd no doubt tell her later, that his pensive mood had nothing to do with her, and decided to give him the news that she knew would cheer him up.

'Guy?' Turning back to face him, she took a deep breath. 'About what you said before...' She swallowed hard, taking a deep breath before she plunged in. 'I was wondering if you wanted to come over for dinner tonight.'

'I can't tonight.' Guy shook his head, then attempted to soften it with a smile. 'I've got all this paperwork to catch up on, and Maternity might ring and ask me to come and translate.'

'OK…' Madison deliberately kept her smile in place, tried to convince herself that it was no big deal, but somehow failed. Switch could ring him on his mobile and since when had paperwork come before them?

'Is Emily out tonight?' Guy asked.

Madison shook her head, blinking back tears, determined not to cry. 'No, I thought you might, you know, come for dinner and…' Her voice trailed off and she ached for him to fill the horrible silence, to somehow acknowledge the magnitude of what she was saying. But still he said nothing.

'You're not worried about the director's position, are you?' Madison tentatively asked, knowing she had hit a nerve when his shoulders stiffened slightly. She inwardly breathed a sigh of relief that it wasn't her that was the problem. 'Guy, the role's yours, Terrence practically said as much, but they can't just give it to you without going through the motions, you know that. Come for dinner tonight, don't worry about it.'

'It's not that simple.' Finally he looked at her, and Madison realized it was the first time his eyes had met hers since she'd stepped into the office. Suddenly she was filled with a sense of foreboding, suddenly all the doubts and fears that she'd pushed aside seemed to be aligning. She ached for him to put her out of her misery, to say something to quell the mounting unease within her, but as Guy finally spoke, Madison felt as if her insides were crumbling, felt her newly found confidence rapidly diminishing as her worst fears were confirmed.

'I'm not sure that I want it, Madison.' Guy's eyes held hers. 'It's a three-year contract.'

'Three years is a long time,' Madison croaked, amazed that somehow she was managing to look at him without crying. 'It's a big commitment. And so is coming to dinner,' Madison added. 'So is coming to my house and meeting my daughter properly.'

'You think I don't know that?' Anguished eyes held hers.

'So what was all that about before, Guy, when you said that you knew what you wanted?'

'Things have changed.'

'You mean I've come round,' Madison said bitterly. 'Finally you've won me over, got me to admit how deeply I feel, and now you're not quite sure that it's what you want after all. Is it the thrill of the chase with you, Guy?'

'You're being unreasonable, Madison,' Guy snapped. 'I just need to think about things. Applications have to be in by Monday. I need to sit down and work out what it is that I want.'

'You still don't know?' Madison asked, unable now to keep an edge of bitterness out of her voice. 'After all we've shared recently, you still don't really know what it is that you want?'

'No,' Guy admitted, his word a brutal slap to her paling cheeks. 'It's not you, Madison, it's me. Maybe it's in the genes.' He was talking faster now, trying to sweeten the bitter pill she was attempting to swallow, but her throat constricted around it, scarcely able to believe that Guy was doing this to her, to them. 'My mum's in her fifties and still drifting around the world, trying to work out what she wants from life. Maybe I take after her more than I thought.'

'Maybe you do,' Madison responded, her lips taut, her face a stricken mask of dignity as she dredged up her inner resources to hold back the tears, to escape this appalling situation with some sense of self intact. 'Maybe you're right to be cautious, Guy. Because as much as I've enjoyed our time together, as much as it's been good, your words make sense. I'm not sure you're what I want for Emily.' She saw his jaw tighten, a rapid blink as he processed her words. 'Emily needs more stability than I think you'd ever be able to give, so perhaps it is better that we end things now before a five-year-old girl gets involved in all this.'

'Perhaps it is,' Guy said, and it wasn't Madison who walked away but Guy. Standing up, he headed around the desk and past her, walked out of his office and into the department. As easily as that he walked away from all they had shared, all the potential that had been there, drifted out of her life as quickly as he'd drifted in, leaving Madison shocked and reeling.

If Mark's death had been hard, it had been a mere practice run. Guy walking away from her like that was sheer, undiluted hell…

Mark had left her in financial ruins, Mark had left her

with a one-year-old child and a lifetime of mess to sort out.

But Guy had actually broken her heart.

CHAPTER NINE

'THE kitchen looks great,' Madison said as she walked down the hall to Helen's brand-new, fully renovated kitchen, leaving Emily in the lounge, playing with Richard. 'Matthew's done a great job!'

'There's nothing left to renovate.' Helen grinned. 'I've got new bathroom cupboards and more shelves than I can fill. I guess it's time to tell Richard.'

'I guess it is.' Madison smiled, recalling Emily's conversation in the car a few weeks ago. 'He mightn't be that shocked that you and Matthew are dating.'

'I hope not.' Helen let out a long tired breath. 'At least he's really got to know Matthew and his daughter, what with all the time he's spent here, supposedly fixing up the place. I'm just scared of taking that final step.'

'I know,' Madison agreed. 'And you're right to be cautious, but Matthew's lovely. He wants this as much as you do…' She tried so hard to be positive, tried so hard to push her own pain aside, but even two weeks after Guy's rejection the pain was just too raw. Her emotions bubbled to the surface and she bit hard on her lip to hold back the ever-threatening tears. Helen reached across her very new, very modern kitchen bench and held her best friend's hand.

'You're better off without him,' Helen said for the hundredth time. 'He was never going to settle, Madison, and, as hard as it's been, you know it was better to find out now than in twelve months' time when Emily was head over heels and wanting to call him Dad.'

'I know,' Madison said, again for the hundredth time. She pulled her hand away after a grateful squeeze and sipped her mug of hot chocolate, wondering when the pain would subside. Wondering how, with Emily and Richard playing happily in the lounge room and her best friend chatting away to her, still she felt this appalling loneliness that quite simply wouldn't leave.

'You said right from the beginning that he was un-reliable.'

She had, but even at this late stage, even when it was irrefutably over and she had every reason to forget him, Madison still couldn't bring herself to do it, because in doing so she would be denying just how wonderful Guy had been for her, the beauty they had shared. And as deep as her pain was, as bitter and as torturous as the ending had been, she still didn't regret it.

Could never regret letting Guy into her life, even though it only had been for a short while.

'At least I don't have to see him any more,' Madison gulped, taking strength from her warm drink. 'He finished work yesterday.'

'Did he say goodbye at least?'

Madison shook her head then gave a small shrug. 'A generic goodbye was the best he could do. He gave a speech, wished the whole department well, but there were certainly no last-minute poignant words. He didn't even look up from the patient he was with when I left.'

'I thought you were going to talk to him, try and find out why at least. Maybe if you told him how much you're hurting…'

'He knows how much I'm hurting.' Madison almost shouted it, then clapped her hand over her mouth, holding it all in just as she always had.

'You're a very good actress, Madison,' Helen said softly. 'Maybe he thinks you're relieved. Maybe if you tell him that you didn't mean what you said about him not being right for Emily…'

'There isn't any point.' For a second she crumpled, dug in her bag for a tissue and blew her nose, before somehow composing herself. 'Because even if I didn't mean it, the simple truth is that Guy wants to leave. We weren't enough to make him want to stay.'

'When does he fly out?'

Madison glanced at her watch. 'In a few hours.'

Even the thought made her tremble inside. Already he'd be nearly on his way to the airport, heading off to another country that needed a doctor but leaving behind a woman and a family, who however hard it had been to admit it, surely needed him, too?

'Have you had any luck getting a new director?'

'Not much,' Madison answered. 'No one really

comes close to Gerard, or Guy come to that. As much as it galls me to admit it, he really is an amazing doctor. He's leaving a big hole and goodness only knows how we're going to fill it.'

'You will,' Helen said firmly, and Madison knew she wasn't talking about the department, knew she was referring to Madison's personal life, but Madison shook her head.

'No, Helen, I won't,' Madison said firmly. 'I'm so over relationships it's not funny. However…' She forced a smile, forced herself to take yet another painful step forward. 'I learnt a lot from Guy. I have been way too wrapped up in providing a stable future. Now I'm going to concentrate on me—and Emily, too, of course…'

'Hey,' Helen broke in. 'You don't have to justify yourself to me. I know that Emily comes first.'

'She does.' Madison nodded. 'And for that reason she needs a mum who's got a life. A full and happy life. A mum who goes out every now and then, who has friends dropping by and is happy in her work. I'm actually thinking of resigning from being NUM.'

'Really? I thought you loved it.'

'I love the pay and I love the hours, but if I have to sit through another meeting trying to shave more money from the linen budget or working out how to reduce the agency nurse bill, I think I'll go crazy. I want to nurse, I want to be out there doing what I'm trained for, and I honestly think I'll be happier for it. I've no idea how I'm going to juggle the shift work, but—'

'I've been thinking about going full time,' Helen

broke in. 'There's a couple of full-time vacancies on the surgical ward for day staff. All these trips to the beauty parlor, clothes and sexy underwear are setting me back a fortune. Now Richard's at school I want my life back, and nursing's a big part of it.'

'Me, too,' Madison agreed, a spark of hope flaring inside her.

'We could help each other,' Helen ventured slowly, neither woman wanting to push, neither woman wanting to burden the other, but both thinking exactly the same thing. 'We could work out our rosters and help each other.'

'We could,' Madison said, blinking at a future that, despite the pain, suddenly looked brighter.

She was going to be OK.

'Hey,' Madison said, as both women sat grinning like Cheshire cats. 'How about I ring that babysitting agency we've always talked about using and book someone very suitable for Emily and Richard some time next week? We can go out for a drink.'

'And a movie.' Helen grinned. 'Something sizzling hot that no parent in their right mind would take a kid to see! We could book for the fancy bit of the movies where they bring you food and drinks.'

'Sounds good.' Standing up, Madison smoothed down her skirt and, pulling out her compact, put on a slick of lipstick. 'Now, I'd better go and see Yvonne. I shouldn't be too long. She just wants to run by me a couple of ideas she's had.'

'Take as long as you like,' Helen said. 'Actually, why

don't you just let Emily stay here tonight? Go home after you've seen Yvonne and have a big bath and an even bigger glass of wine.

'A big cry, too,' Helen added. 'Get him out of your system.'

'You're sure?' Madison asked, not sure she should be so pleased at the prospect of bawling her eyes out but infinitely grateful for Helen's insight. The last couple of weeks had been torture, facing Guy at work, dealing with Emily at home, trying to function on a tank that was running on empty.

After kissing Emily goodbye and warning her to be good, Madison hauled herself into the car and braced herself for the prospect of facing Yvonne, of feigning excitement over the scholarship project. Why did everything feel such an effort these days? Even her usually immaculate car looked as if a whirlwind had hit it inside. Sand from the beach, lolly wrappers, Emily's library book and a couple of toys littered the back seat. She really had to get her life back on track, really had to stop dwelling on the past and look to the future. But the secure future she'd longingly envisioned didn't seem quite so appealing any more.

'Thank you for coming, Madison.'

The perfect hostess, Yvonne took Madison's jacket and ushered her through to the lounge, pouring her guest a drink before joining her on the sofa. 'As I told you, I've been in touch with a couple of the AID agencies Gerard had been affiliated with and I've had some very promising responses.' She held out two letters to Madison, which she read in thoughtful silence, read about the devastating conditions people were enduring, the ray of hope that Gerard had offered. 'These two centres in particular Gerard was extremely fond of. The first is an orphanage, mainly consisting of children who have lost their parents to AIDS and most of the children themselves are HIV positive. A doctor coming in regularly, bringing medication and regimes, would mean so much to their lives.'

'It would,' Madison agreed, tears filling her eyes as she stared at the enclosed photos, the gaunt, hopeless faces of the children looking back at her.

'The other is a medical centre. Currently it has a doctor who visits for two days once every six months.' She handed over some more photos, more painful than the last if that was possible. As Madison gazed at the pictures she took in the pregnant women lining up for their one chance at antenatal care, the supposed hospital beds filled with sick-looking patients who never even got to see a doctor but were tended by the locals and a couple of nurses, who were doing their best in what could only be described as the most appalling of conditions.

'They're both marvelous causes. I'm sure many doctors would love the opportunity to work at either of these places.'

'Now I have to decide which one.' Yvonne let out a strained sigh. 'I've been going over and over in my mind which one Gerard would have chosen, but I think even he would have had trouble making up his mind. What do you think, Madison?'

'Me?' Madison said helplessly.

'You.' Yvonne nodded. 'I'd really appreciate your input.'

And it was almost impossible because Madison knew that her input would count. Staring at the pictures, rereading the letters, she tried and failed to be objective. She was performing a nightmarish triage where more lives were at stake than she could even fathom.

'I think,' Madison whispered, overwhelmed by the responsibility, overwhelmed at even the prospect that her next words might have some influence, 'it's almost impossible to decide between the two when they're both such desperate causes. These people all deserve medical care…'

'Go on,' Yvonne said. 'Tell me what you're thinking.'

'The clinic.' Madison closed her eyes in regret, feeling personally responsible for those poor desperate children, scarcely able to believe she was turning her back on them. 'Is there any way we could help both?' she asked desperately.

'No,' Yvonne said regretfully. 'Why do you think the clinic would be a more deserving choice?' Seeing Madison tense, she rephrased her question. 'Why do you think we should choose the clinic?'

'Because we can do more good there,' Madison tentatively replied. 'Looking at the figures in the letters I've read, there's a huge number of people with very limited medical help. A full-time doctor would change that, would save hundreds, thousands of lives even. And as worthy as the other cause is, I think working in a hospital will be more of a draw card for us to recruit doctors.'

'I agree,' Yvonne said. 'It's not an easy choice, though, is it?'

'It's a terrible choice,' Madison gulped. 'But I'm trying hard to think what Gerard would have done. And I truly want us to utilize the resources wisely…'

'For the greater good,' Yvonne said fondly. 'You're exactly right. As much of a soft touch as he could be, as much as he adored children and would have loved to have helped every last one, at the end of the day he was a doctor and his mission was to save or improve as many lives as he could. I think expanding this clinic, making it into a hospital, would enable him to do that. Here, let me show you something.'

Pulling out a photo album, she began leafing through the pictures with Madison. Both women looked at the images of a much younger Gerard surrounded by a team of nurses, a tiny baby in his arms and a huge contented smile on his face. 'He did have a huge soft spot for children and this way we'll still be helping them. Those women you saw in the photo deserve antenatal care and help if anything goes wrong in delivery. Their babies deserve to have a doctor to treat them, to give vaccinations, all the things we take for granted.'

'I know,' Madison agreed, warming to her choice, seeing clearly for the first time the full scale of the impact that this scholarship programme might bring. 'He loved kids. The place could be full to the rafters, the waiting room and every trolley filled with patients, and Gerard would hear a child crying and stop what he was doing to find out why—ask us why on earth a child was being left in pain.'

'That was Gerard.' Yvonne nodded. 'There aren't too many doctors like him any more.'

'Guy Boyd's the same,' Madison said unthinkingly, and it had nothing to do with the fact that she adored him. Quite simply she was speaking the truth, but clearly she'd said the wrong thing. The amicable conversation stilled and the atmosphere grew so tense suddenly it could have been cut with a knife.

'Guy Boyd's nothing like Gerard,' Yvonne snarled. 'Heatherton Hospital will be far better off without him. He's a drifter—he never had any intention of staying on,' Yvonne pointed out. 'I've known Guy for a couple of years and I can't say I've taken to him. He's too irresponsible for words, drifting from one place to the next, just like his—' Yvonne's mouth snapped closed and as Madison turned a page of the photo album she knew why. Looking down at a photo, Madison stared into two very familiar hazel eyes, stared at fair hair flopping over Gerard's forehead, took in the sculptured cheekbones and long straight nose, features she knew because they were etched on her heart. Only it had nothing to do with a boss she had admired, it had nothing in fact to do with Gerard Dalton. The face staring back at her was Guy's.

A million scattered thoughts that had always been

there, just never acknowledged, aligned in an instant as the truth finally hit home.

That spark of recognition when she had first met him.

The fondness in Gerard's voice when he spoke of Guy.

The pain she had witnessed on Guy's face at the funeral.

Yvonne's animosity, her fear that Madison had somehow found out the truth when Gerard had collapsed… Suddenly it was crystal clear.

Guy was Gerard's son!

'I really ought to get going, Yvonne.' Not by a flicker did Madison change her expression. Somehow she kept her voice light as she snapped the photo album closed and stood up.

'So soon,' Yvonne said. 'I was hoping to talk some more. I know Gerard valued your opinion. He'd want you to be involved with this.'

'I want to be involved, too, but I have to get back to my babysitter, Yvonne,' Madison said apologetically. 'But if it's OK with you, I'll come over again soon.'

'You do that.' Standing, Yvonne saw her to the door, waved her off. Madison attempted a rather shaky U-turn, but instead of turning left at the lights, instead of heading back to her home, she turned right, the bright lights of the hospital beckoning her. Only this time she bypassed Emergency, drove her car through the grounds and to the back of the complex to the doctors' residences. Questioning the wisdom of her actions, she raced up the stairs, her shoes clattering on the polished stairs. She had no idea what she was going to say. She was just filled with a need to see Guy, a need to tell him she knew, that maybe she finally understood.

'You've missed him.' A doctor she vaguely recognized peered out of his door as Madison rapped loudly on Guy's. 'He left a couple of hours ago.'

'For the airport?' Madison checked, trying to hold back her tears, nodding her thanks when the doctor nodded back. She raced back down the stairs and headed for her car.

It should have been a half-hour drive to the airport, but everything seemed to be against her—red lights, night roadworks, even the security guards at the airport, who told Madison in no uncertain terms that there was no way she was leaving her car at the entrance, that even if she only needed five minutes she'd have to go to the short-term car park.

Which took five minutes to find!

And five minutes to find a space.

Her lungs bursting, she raced through the multistorey car park. Bypassing the lift, she raced down the stairs, scanning the unfamiliar signs, racing towards International Departures but knowing she was already too late. As she skidded in she frantically scanned the terminal for a sign of him. She eyed the departure and arrivals screens and only then did she acknowledge that it was useless. She didn't even know where he was going, only that surely he had left already. And there was no one for a man like Guy to say goodbye to.

The departures board whirred into action, the white letters spinning rapidly, updating the information as Madison just stood there. She watched as several words changed from boarding to departed and finally acknowledged that she'd lost him.

That she'd left it too late.

'Looks like I'm going to miss it!'

Hearing his deep voice, the last voice she had ever expected to hear again, Madison jumped. Turning around abruptly, her tear-streaked face gaped as she saw Guy standing before her. His backpack was on the floor beside him, his ticket and boarding pass in hand, and all she could think of was that he was beautiful, and all she could be at that moment was grateful.

That, for whatever reason, he was here.

That, for whatever reason, now at least she would get her chance to say goodbye properly—to admit the truth, that, however impossible, however improbable their relationship might be, she would always, quite simply, love him.

'Guy.' Her voice was a croak, her first instinct to fall into his arms, but she held back, terrified of crowding him, terrified that if she moved, if she blinked, if she spoke even, somehow he might just disappear.

'I couldn't go, Madison.' Guy's voice wasn't exactly strong either. Pain was etched on every feature, crushed, devastated eyes held hers. 'I couldn't go without saying goodbye. I know that we're not right for each other, but I couldn't leave it like that.'

'I know,' Madison gulped, because she did. Knew

that even if they couldn't make it, what they had had was worth acknowledging, that what they'd shared was worth that much at least.

'I wanted to explain to you why I was leaving, but I can't. You have to understand that. I promised I wouldn't say anything, I promised Yvonne, I promised Gerard…'

Slowly she walked towards him, watched as this proud, remote man attempted to reach out to her one final time. She met him halfway. 'You don't have to break that promise, Guy, I've already worked it out. Gerard was your father, wasn't he?'

And when finally he nodded, Madison could only wonder how she'd taken so long to see it. It wasn't just their features that were the same, but their dignity, their poise, their compassion.

The loudspeaker announcing departures startled them both, and Guy gestured to the revolving doors. 'Shall we take this outside?'

'Have you really missed your flight?'

'Probably.' He shrugged. 'There'll be one tomorrow.'

She reluctantly nodded, accepted that he was leaving and reminded herself that she was grateful to at least say goodbye. She waited for him to pick up his belongings and followed him outside.

'When did you find out?'

'Two years ago.' Guy blew out the breath he had been holding. 'Mum would never tell me who my father was. Sometimes she said that she didn't really know, but finally she admitted that when she was a junior doctor she'd taken a gap year and gone to work overseas. That's where they met. They had a brief fling and I was the result.'

'Did Gerard know?' Madison asked, but Guy shook his head.

'Mum chose not to tell him. She wanted to go it alone—I told you she was ahead of her time. I contacted him a couple of years ago and we were both blown away by how much we had in common—not just how we looked, but the fact that we were both doctors, both interested in AID work. Gerard was appalled that he hadn't known about me and wanted to make up for all the lost years. The only problem was Yvonne. Even though it had happened years before they were together, Yvonne simply couldn't accept that he'd had a child by another woman. She was terrified of people finding out and what everyone would think.'

'But what about Gerard?' Madison asked. 'He wasn't like that.'

'He loved Yvonne and he loved his kids. He felt as guilty as hell for all the pain he was causing them. In the end I told them all that I didn't want to cause trouble, that I'd never reveal who I was. I had just wanted to get to know Gerard better. That was the only reason I looked him up—to fill in a few blanks. I never wanted to disrupt anyone's life so I headed back overseas, just stayed in touch via e-mail and the odd phone call.'

'Until the consultant's position came up,' Madison said for him. 'What made you change your mind?'

'It was Gerard's idea. He wanted to get to know me better, too, and I have to admit I jumped at the chance. Only Yvonne wasn't at all keen, but he finally won her around, though we both agreed that we'd never reveal we were related. Gerard finally got her to understand that we just wanted the chance to spend some time together. I promised Yvonne it would only be for six months, that I just wanted to get to know my…Gerard.'

'You can say it, Guy,' Madison whispered, but he shook his head.

'No, Madison, I can't. Yvonne doesn't want me around, she's made it very clear.'

'She can't make you leave!' Madison gasped. 'Surely you know that.'

'She can't make me leave,' Guy agreed, 'but she can pull the plug on the scholarship.'

'She wouldn't,' Madison gasped, but Guy just stared back at her, hopelessness etched on every feature.

'When I told her that Gerard had died, I promised her that I wouldn't breathe a word, but that now more than ever I had to stay on at the hospital, that they couldn't lose both the consultant and director in one day. I thought she was coming around to the idea. I was discreet at the funeral…'

Madison's mind flicked back, marveling at the strength of him, that in the midst of his own very real, very personal grief somehow he had reached out and comforted her.

'I even thought she was worried I was going to contest the will. I swore I wouldn't—that the last thing I wanted was Gerard's money—and for a while things went quiet. I got on with work and met you…'

'What happened, Guy?' Madison's voice was firm now, needing to know what had happened, what had made this beautiful, honourable man change his mind.

'After that meeting, when she asked to have a word, Yvonne told me that I had two weeks to leave, that if I didn't move away then she wasn't going to go ahead with the scholarship programme.

'It was Gerard's dream,' Guy whispered. 'You said yourself nothing would have made him more proud than for this to happen. How could I live with myself if I stayed and she went ahead and removed the programme? It's not just Gerard I'm thinking of but the hospital, too, and all the kids that it would help.'

'Gerard would never have wanted it this way,' Madison said. 'She's asking you to walk out on your career, on a life…' Madison swallowed hard. 'And on me.'

'You don't want me,' Guy pointed out, and Madison blinked back at him, utterly bemused. 'Maybe I am a drifter, maybe it is all in the genes. Look at my mother—'

'Look at your father,' Madison interrupted. 'Look at that side of the gene pool, Guy. And I've never stopped wanting you, not even for a second. Why do you think I'm here? Why do you think I'm standing in an airport terminal at this time of night?'

'To say goodbye?'

'To beg you to stay,' Madison cried. 'Guy, when I

said that about you not being right for Emily, that was me just being defensive. You'd make a wonderful father…' Clapping her hand over her mouth Madison's eyes widened, stunned at what she had said, terrified at what she had just confessed, but Guy for the first time since she'd seen him that night was smiling. Smiling that delicious lazy smile.

'Is that a proposal?'

'I don't know,' Madison croaked. 'But here's one for you—go and tell Yvonne that you won't be black-mailed. Go and tell Yvonne that you're staying where you belong—because, whether or not Emily and I are in the picture, you know that you belong here now. You know that the department needs you…' She was finding her voice now, anger growing inside for what Yvonne had done. 'Tell her that she cannot threaten you and she cannot influence you.'

'It's not that easy—'

'But it is,' Madison broke in, fighting not just for herself but for what was right. 'I could just about take losing you if you didn't want to be here, if you wanted to move on with your life, but I'm not going to lose you all over again because Yvonne has decided that she wants you out of the picture.'

'We could move somewhere else,' Guy suggested, his eyes imploring her to understand. 'The AID work would still go ahead. I'd take care of you and Emily.'

It sounded easy but it wasn't, and even as he said it Madison saw the hopelessness drift back into his eyes as she shook her head.

'I've got a life, Guy, a life I've fought hard to keep. And I'm not going to give it away for Yvonne.'

'I understand.' Utterly defeated, he nodded, his hand reaching for his backpack, but Madison hadn't finished yet.

'Guy, if we stay together, one day we might have to move, one day we might even want to move, but this is just plain wrong!'

'We're talking thousands of lives that could be saved, Madison.' Guy was shouting now. 'We're talking about my father's dream. It can't just be about me or even us.'

'What would Gerard have wanted?' Madison asked, watching as he stiffened. 'What would Gerard have really wanted you to do, Guy? He was an honourable man, he fought for what was right, and he wouldn't have wanted this. You're his son, and nothing Yvonne can do can change that fact.

'Tell her.' Madison stared defiantly back at him. 'Tell her that you're staying. Tell her that if she pulls the plug on the scholarship then she's the one killing Gerard's dream, not you.'

And her words must have sunk in because the backpack was down on the floor again. Tension was etched on Guy's face as he made the most difficult decision of his life.

'We'll tell her together,' Madison rasped. 'And then you're coming home.'

'Home?' She heard the question in his single word and it made her want to weep. This loyal, beautiful man didn't even know what that word really meant, and she realized that although he'd drifted, responsibility was ingrained into him, and that there really was a man in this world she could actually trust.

Actually love.

'Home,' Madison said again. 'To Emily and me.'

His hand raked through his hair as she bravely went on. 'We'll have to introduce you slowly. I can't just walk in and say that this is the man—'

'Who you're going to spend the rest of your life with,' Guy finished for her. The tension left his face as, in the end, that most difficult decision was made easy.

'Come home with me now, Guy,' Madison said, not a single doubt in her mind. And as his lips found hers and she melted into his arms, let him hold her, let him love her, Madison knew that they would be together, that both of them had found peace.

'Can I see Emily?' Guy asked, breaking away, staring down at her with love blazing from his eyes.

'Not yet,' Madison whispered. 'Because—'

'I understand,' Guy interrupted. 'Madison, whenever you're ready is fine by me. I'm not going to rush you.'

'If you'd let me finish.' Madison smiled. 'I was about to say that maybe it could wait until tomorrow as I've got a babysitter for the night. The house is empty, I thought that maybe we could spend a little time…' She gave a very wicked, very tiny grin. 'Of course, I could ring Helen and tell her we're coming. If you really want to meet Emily tonight, it's no trouble to arrange it.'

'Tomorrow will be fine.' Guy laughed.

'It will be,' Madison said, and she wasn't talking about Emily now but about them, about the future and everything it held. 'Tomorrow will be fine, but tonight's…' She nestled back into his arms, reluctant to let him go for even a moment.

'Tonight's about us.'

EPILOGUE

'THOSE tablets can make you a bit nauseous at first.'

Guy came into the bathroom and Madison wished he hadn't. Even after six months together and having obtained a closeness she had never imagined possible, there was still a desire to maintain just a hint of mystery—and being head first down the loo wasn't exactly going to achieve that!

'I'll be out in a moment.' Madison grimaced, standing up and splashing her face with water, staring at the beastly packet of antimalaria tablets sitting beside the bathroom sink.

'I'm fine now.' A touch pale, Madison came out of the bathroom and perched herself on the bed next to Guy, who was looking at her with concerned eyes. 'I wasn't actually sick, I just felt a bit nauseous.'

'It will soon wear off,' Guy assured her. 'And it's necessary. The last thing you want to come home with is a dose of malaria. You have to remember to take them each day and for a month after we get home…' His voice shifted slightly and Madison watched as his gaze drifted around the bedroom.

Their bedroom, in their home. The house she had fought so hard to keep, to protect, a real home now. Full of love and laughter and just a touch too much clutter perhaps, but Madison wouldn't have traded it for anything. And she knew, as Guy stared hard at the massive backpacks bulging on the bedroom floor, his face suddenly pensive, that for the first time in his life he didn't want to leave, didn't want to move on even for a little while.

But he had to.

Gerard's dream was taking shape. This time tomorrow they would be boarding a plane for a two-week visit to the rudimentary medical centre that would soon become a hospital, bringing with them the first batch of supplies. They would oversee the first stages of building, laying the foundations for a future of hope.

'How's Emily?' Guy asked, his voice concerned. 'She was a bit teary about us going last night. Madison, if you want to stay with her then that's OK with me. There will be other trips—lots of them, no doubt!'

'Emily will be fine,' Madison answered. 'In fact, I think she's even more excited about the hospital than we are, and she's looking forward to two weeks of being spoiled by her grandparents. I explained to her this morning that next time we go, she'll definitely come. Once there are some basic facilities there's no reason why she shouldn't come and see for herself the work you're doing.'

'We're all doing,' Guy corrected. 'I can't believe how much everyone has got behind the project.

Yvonne was telling me that her church group is holding a sausage sizzle in the high street next week. I almost wish I were here to see it. I can't exactly imagine Yvonne with a pair of tongs and a mountain of greasy sausages.'

'I can.' Madison laughed. 'She's really changed, hasn't she?'

'Completely,' Guy agreed. 'You know, as much as she hurt me over the last couple of years, trying to push me away, trying to pretend I didn't exist, I just couldn't get angry at her. She was just scared of everything falling apart, worried that once people knew that Gerard actually had a past that didn't include her, people would judge her.'

'But they are judging her,' Madison said. 'Only for all the right reasons now. She's a great step-mum! She's really proud of you, and I know Gerard would have been too. It took a lot of courage to stand up to her.'

'Yeah, but if I hadn't had you beside me, I'd never have done it.'

The pensive moment over, Guy stood up and started rolling up a very weary-looking sleeping bag to place in the pile next to Madison's very new, very red one.

'We can zip them up together.' Guy grinned, catching her staring at him.

'I thought you said that at the end of a long day, doing AID work, all you wanted to do was go to sleep.'

'That was before I met you,' Guy said, but his grin faded when she didn't smile back. He took in her pale face and strained features. 'What's wrong, Madison?'

'Nothing,' Madison attempted, but she knew she wasn't fooling anyone.

'You don't want to leave Emily, do you?'

'I actually do want to, and after our talk this morning I think she wants me to go now, too. I just don't think I can.' Fiddling with her fingers she stared down at the simple gold band Guy had proudly placed on her finger a few short weeks ago. She twisted it round and round for a couple of moments before continuing. 'I feel really sick, Guy.'

'It's the tablets.' Guy gave a relieved laugh and sat back down on the bed, his hands pulling apart her tense ones and holding them tight. 'You won't feel like this for long, I promise…'

'It isn't the tablets,' Madison gulped, 'because I didn't take any.'

'Why?'

She could feel his eyes burning into the top of her head but she didn't dare look up. 'I wasn't sure if they were teratogenic…'

'Teratogenic?' Guy's voice was hoarse.

'If the tablets would have any unwanted side effects on the baby—'

'I know what teratogenic means,' Guy broke in. 'It's the baby bit I don't know about. How long have you known?'

'About half an hour,' Madison said. 'I've felt a bit sick for a couple of days and I'm a bit overdue. Before I took anything, I thought it better to check.' Fumbling in her bedside table, she pulled out a plastic pregnancy testing strip and handed it to him. 'It's terrible timing, what with the hospital and everything. I didn't plan…'

'Hey, you sacked your life coach.' Guy smiled, staring at the plastic. 'You've stopped making plans, remember?' His eyes found hers. 'You've started living.'

'But even so!' A wobble of excitement grew inside her as his smile widened. He wrapped her in his arms and hushed her fears.

'We're having a baby!' Guy whispered over and over until finally Madison started to really believe it. Booked flights and ruined schedules didn't matter a scrap. The magnitude of what was happening finally started to hit and later, when he'd loved her all over again, when she was lying in his arms, feeling totally at one with the world, she said what was on both of their minds.

'I wish Gerard could have known.'

'He knows,' Guy said softly. 'That's why you two were so close, that's why he watched out for you— he knew that one day you were going to have his grandchild.'

'Maybe he did,' Madison mused. 'Not consciously, of course, but somewhere deep inside maybe he felt a connection.'

'A connection!' Laughing, propping himself on his elbow, Guy smiled down at her. 'You'll be lighting incense next and telling me you want a natural water birth.'

'Not likely.' Madison grimaced then dug him in the ribs. 'Thanks for reminding me, I'd forgotten all about that part. I'm having every drug on the trolley.'

'What happened to the straight-laced, terribly rigid Madison Walsh I first met?'

'She got lucky.' Madison smiled. 'And then she got happy.'

MILLS & BOON®

Live the emotion

Medical
romance™

THE SURGEON'S PREGNANCY SURPRISE
by Laura MacDonald

At a friend's wedding, Chrissie Paige falls for the best man – fellow surgeon Sean O'Reagan. After one passionate weekend together they go their separate ways. Chrissie can't stop thinking about him. Then she finds that not only is Sean her new boss, but she's pregnant with his child!

A FRENCH DOCTOR AT ABBEYFIELDS
by Abigail Gordon

When Dr Giselle Howard arrives at Abbeyfields she has no intention of leaving her Parisian lifestyle behind. But the welcome she gets from the villagers, not to mention the affection she has for local GP Marc Bannerman and his two young children, creates a bond she can't ignore…

Abigail Gordon charms us with her enchanting depiction of the warmth and community of English village life

IN HIS LOVING CARE *by Jennifer Taylor*

Lewis Cole's life has changed in an instant – he has a daughter! No longer single city surgeon, he's single father and country GP. He's determined to give little Kristy all the love she needs, but there's also room in his heart for beautiful Dr Helen Daniels. Helen, however, needs more – a child of her own…

Bachelor Dads – Single Doctor… Single Father!

On sale 3rd March 2006

Available at WHSmith, Tesco, ASDA, Borders, Eason, Sainsbury's and most bookshops

www.millsandboon.co.uk

0206/03b

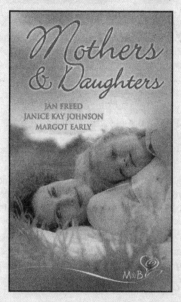

FREE

4 BOOKS AND A SURPRISE GIFT!

We would like to take this opportunity to thank you for reading this Mills & Boon® book by offering you the chance to take FOUR more specially selected titles from the Medical Romance™ series absolutely FREE! We're also making this offer to introduce you to the benefits of the Reader Service™—

- ★ **FREE home delivery**
- ★ **FREE gifts and competitions**
- ★ **FREE monthly Newsletter**
- ★ **Books available before they're in the shops**
- ★ **Exclusive Reader Service offers**

Accepting these FREE books and gift places you under no obligation to buy; you may cancel at any time, even after receiving your free shipment. Simply complete your details below and return the entire page to the address below. You don't even need a stamp!

YES! Please send me 4 free Medical Romance books and a surprise gift. I understand that unless you hear from me, I will receive 6 superb new titles every month for just £2.75 each, postage and packing free. I am under no obligation to purchase any books and may cancel my subscription at any time. The free books and gift will be mine to keep in any case.

M6ZEE

Ms/Mrs/Miss/Mr..................................Initials ....
BLOCK CAPITALS PLEASE

Surname ....

Address ....

....

....Postcode ....

Send this whole page to:
The Reader Service, FREEPOST CN81, Croydon, CR9 3WZ